READ & LISTEN OS MELHORES CONTOS DO SÉCULO XX EM VERSÃO ORIGINAL NA ÍNTEGRA

"Sometimes all we need
is a fine, short story."

martins
Martins Fontes

Alice Munro

The Progress of Love

•

Margaret Atwood

Death by Landscape

Publisher *Evandro Mendonça Martins Fontes*
Coordenação editorial *Anna Dantes*
Produção editorial *Alyne Azuma*
Tradução *Betty Nisembaum*
Preparação *Denise Roberti Camargo*
Revisão *André Albert*
Dinarte Zorzanelli da Silva

Biografias e apresentações *Laura Fernández*
Locução de "The Progress of Love" *Amber Ockrassa*
Locução de "Death by Landscape" *Amber Ockrassa*
Gravação *RecLab*
Técnico *Francesc Gosalves*

Dados Internacionais de Catalogação na Publicação (CIP)
(Câmara Brasileira do Livro, SP, Brasil)

Munro, Alice, 1931-.

The progress of love / Alice Munro. Death by landscape / Margaret Atwood / [tradução Betty Nisembaum]. – 1. ed. – São Paulo : Martins Martins Fontes, 2011.

Título original: The progress of love ; Death by landscape.
Inclui CD.
ISBN 978-85-8063-009-1

1. Contos canadenses I. Atwood, Margaret, 1939-. II. Título. III. Título: Death by landscape.

11-02234 CDD-819.1

Índices para catálogo sistemático:
1. Contos : Literatura canadense 819.1

Av. Dr. Arnaldo, 2076
01255-000 São Paulo SP Brasil
Tel. (11) 3116.0000
info@martinseditora.com.br
www.martinsmartinsfontes.com.br

SUMÁRIO

INTRODUÇÃO

Dê um passo além e leia os clássicos em versão original

Para muitos de nós, ler em versão original supõe um desafio por vezes irrealizável. Habituados a nossa própria língua, ficamos frustrados quando não entendemos todas as palavras de um texto. Quantas vezes deixamos um livro de lado porque não queremos consultar o dicionário a toda hora? Essa consulta (quase sempre obrigatória) se soma ao desconhecimento das referências culturais, à dificuldade de perceber os matizes, a ironia do autor etc. Logo nos aborrecemos por não conseguir compreender a essência do relato e acabamos fechando o livro e buscando a versão traduzida.

Na coleção READ & LISTEN a leitura e audição do texto original produzem experiências tão únicas quanto a de contemplar uma pintura em vez de sua reprodução. Não só se aprende como também se desfruta e assimila o verdadeiro espírito do relato.

Aqui, os leitores podem ter acesso aos melhores contos dos mais respeitados autores de língua inglesa, com as ferramentas necessárias para compreender os textos em sua totalidade.

Foi-se o tempo de ler com o dicionário do lado. Cada conto inclui um extenso glossário para que não seja necessário interromper a leitura. Além de todas as palavras que você pode não entender, ele apresenta referências culturais, deixa claras as nuances e permite compreender todos os toques irônicos de cada conto. Para quem quer praticar a compreensão oral ou simplesmente ouvir o texto enquanto o lê, nada mais simples. Ponha o CD com a versão em áudio dos contos para tocar, sente-se, relaxe e deixe que um locutor nativo conte a história. Porque não há maneira melhor de colocar ao seu alcance essas obras-primas do que rompendo as barreiras que o mantiveram longe delas durante tanto tempo.

Quem tem medo dos clássicos?

E por falar em clássicos... Nossa seleção se guiou por várias premissas: em primeiro lugar, os contos tinham de ser sugestivos e não muito complexos; em segundo lugar, tinham de representar o mundo próprio de cada autor. Clássicos em miniatura, inesquecíveis, os contos desta coleção devem ser lidos com cuidado, degustando cada frase, cada palavra. São obras capazes de transformar seus personagens em alguém conhecido, quase familiar, que poderia ser seu melhor amigo.

Acreditamos que, depois de tanto tempo aprendendo inglês, chegou seu momento de desfrutar. Você merece.

Alice Munro

The Progress of Love

"The word 'gone' seemed full of nothing but a deep relief and even an excitement—the excitement you feel when a door closes and your house sinks back to normal and you let yourself loose into all the free space around you."

BIOGRAFIA

Alice Munro

Alice Munro (Wingham, Canadá, 1931) tinha 19 anos quando publicou seu primeiro conto, "The Dimensions of a Shadow". Nessa época, ela saía com um rapaz tímido, James Munro, ainda se chamava Alice Laidlaw, frequentava a Universidade de Western Ontario e pagava os seus estudos servindo bebidas em um bar. Alice, que fora criada em uma fazenda no povoado frio de Wingham, deixou tudo para trás um ano após a publicação de seu primeiro conto para casar-se com James, o rapaz tímido.

Mudaram-se para Vancouver e tiveram três filhas (Sheila, Catherine e Jenny) entre 1953 e 1957. Uma delas, Catherine, morreu pouco depois de nascer, levando Alice e James a uma profunda depressão da qual a escritora escapou graças a seus contos. Apesar de sua primeira compilação, *Dance of the Happy Shades* [Dança das sombras felizes], só ter chegado às livrarias uma década depois, em 1968, Alice nunca deixou de escrever. Naquele tempo, ela o fazia atrás do balcão da livraria Munro's Books, que o casal abriu em Victoria, cidade para a qual se mudaram em 1963, três anos antes de nascer Andrea, sua quarta filha.

Assim, Alice Munro não era senão uma simpática livreira do interior quando ganhou seu primeiro Governor General's Award (o prêmio mais prestigioso do seu Canadá natal) pela sua primeira antologia de contos, a já citada *Dance of the Happy Shades*. Três anos depois, em 1971, chegaria a sua única tentativa de romance – que na realidade não era outra coisa senão os contos disfarçados com "algo mais" –, chamada *Lives of Girls and Women* [Vidas de meninas e mulheres], que foi adaptada para a televisão em 1994.

Um ano depois, seu casamento com James Munro tinha ficado no passado, e Alice regressou a Ontário, onde se tornou professora titular da universidade na qual havia conhecido o rapaz tímido. Em 1976 voltou a se casar, dessa vez com um geógrafo chamado Gerald Fremlin. Juntos se mudaram para uma fazenda nos arredores de Clinton (na mesma Ontário). Como aquilo não combinava com eles, venderam a fazenda e voltaram para a cidade, onde Alice criou uma nova antologia de contos, *Who Do You Think You Are?* [Quem você pensa que é?], que lhe valeu seu segundo Governor General's Award. O terceiro chegaria em 1986, com a publicação de *The Progress of Love* [O progresso do amor], com toda certeza sua obra-prima, ao lado de *Fugitiva*, uma de suas mais recentes coleções de contos. Antes de isso ocorrer, Munro deu uma pequena volta ao mundo (Austrália, China, Escandinávia) entre 1979 e 1982. Desde então não deixou de escrever, de ganhar prêmios e de somar fãs ilustres (um deles, o magnífico escritor norte-americano Jonathan Franzen, ficou tão fascinado por sua prosa que a única crítica que conseguiu fazer foi: "Leiam Munro! Leiam Munro!").

Os contos de Munro (tão profundos que se tornam, como no caso de "The Progress of Love", romances em miniatura) são povoados por personagens que se deparam com si mesmos no espelho um dia e se sentem crianças presas em um mundo de adultos. Ambientados frequentemente em Huron (Ontário), são considerados o expoente máximo do chamado gótico sulista *made in* Ontário.

APRESENTAÇÃO DO CONTO

The Progress of Love

"Mamãe estava brincando", diz Beryl a sua irmã Marietta uma tarde qualquer, em uma cafeteria. Marietta não acredita que sua mãe estava brincando quando subiu naquela cadeira, colocou uma corda ao redor do pescoço e ameaçou pular. "Vá buscar seu pai, quero falar com ele", foi o que ela disse. E Marietta, apenas uma criança, se pôs a correr até o bar onde sabia, com toda certeza, que ia encontrá-lo. Mas não o encontrou, e quando voltou, com o coração na boca, achando que veria a mãe pendurada na viga da cozinha, encontrou-a tomando uma xícara de café com a vizinha. Um milhão de anos depois, a sua irmã Beryl lhe disse que na realidade sua mãe "estava brincando". Era isso mesmo? O seu pai a quis? Seu retraído pai as quis? Por que, então, fez Marietta devolver tudo que ele tinha gasto com ela antes de se casar com o rapaz pelo qual estava apaixonada? A protagonista de "The Progress of Love" é o fantasma de Marietta, traçado pelas lembranças da sua filha, que nasceu e cresceu em uma fazenda, foi terrivelmente pobre e fugiu das duas coisas – a fazenda e a pobreza – assim que foi possível (ainda que a alternativa fosse instalar-se na cidade podre e virar camareira); mesmo sentindo que partia o coração da sua mãe, não tinha outro remédio.

Incluído na antologia de mesmo título, "The Progress of Love" é um dos melhores exemplos do universo Munro. Considerada por muitos a melhor contista contemporânea, e frequentemente comparada com a brutal Flannery O'Connor, Munro devolveu à literatura rural o brilho perdido após a desaparição de O'Connor, John Steinbeck e mesmo William Faulkner, e o fez trocando o Sul pelo Norte, a estrada poeirenta da América Profunda pela fazenda gelada de um povoado canadense em Ontário, onde ela mesma cresceu. Construídos com maestria, semelhante às bonecas russas (em tudo o que conta, Munro esconde algo, a peça-chave que permite entender o conjunto é revelada apenas nas últimas linhas), os contos de Alice Munro são de uma simplicidade e economia quase poéticas (ela brinca com o tempo, constrói suas histórias por meio de *flashbacks*, mas o faz com frases de bagagem leve). Introduzem o leitor a um universo fechado, claustrofóbico, onde reina a mulher forte e, neste caso mais do que nunca, os princípios, o amor, o respeito e, sim, também o ódio.

Não perca a versão lida da história, incluída no CD. É outra maneira de saborear esta prosa sonora de Alice Munro. A história da menina que recebe a ligação do seu pai e escuta o seu "acho que a mamãe se foi" esconde outra história maior. É como a boneca russa ao esconder a sua pequena e sorridente irmã de plástico, que quase sempre traz consigo uma nova história.

LAURA FERNÁNDEZ

The Progress of Love

I GOT A CALL AT WORK, and it was my father. This was not long after I was divorced and started in the real-estate office[1]. Both of my boys were in school. It was a hot enough day in September.

My father was so polite, even in the family. He took time to ask me how I was. Country manners[2]. Even if somebody phones up to tell you your house is burning down, they ask first how you are.

"I'm fine," I said. "How are you?"

"Not so good, I guess," said my father, in his old way—apologetic but self-respecting[3]. "I think your mother's gone."

I knew that "gone" meant "dead". I knew that. But for a second or so I saw my mother in her black straw hat[4] setting off down the lane[5]. The word "gone" seemed full of nothing but a deep relief and even an excitement—the excitement you feel when a door closes and your house sinks back to normal[6] and you let yourself loose[7] into all the free space around you. That was in my father's voice too—behind the apology, a queer sound like a gulped breath[8]. But my

1 **real-estate office:** imobiliária • 2 **country manners:** os bons modos das pessoas do campo • 3 **apologetic but self-respecting:** com expressão de pesar, mas com amor próprio • 4 **straw hat:** chapéu de palha • 5 **setting off down the lane:** se afastando pelo caminho • 6 **sinks back to normal:** volta à normalidade • 7 **you let yourself loose:** você relaxa • 8 **a queer sound like a gulped breath:** um barulho estranho como o de uma respiração presa

mother hadn't been a burden[1]—she hadn't been sick a day—and far from feeling relieved at her death, my father took it hard[2]. He never got used to living alone, he said. He went into the Netterfield County Home quite willingly[3].

He told me how he found my mother on the couch[4] in the kitchen when he came in at noon. She had picked[5] a few tomatoes, and was setting them on the windowsill to ripen[6]; then she must have felt weak, and lain down. Now, telling this, his voice went wobbly[7]—meandering[8], as you would expect—in his amazement[9]. I saw in my mind the couch, the old quilt[10] that protected it, right under the phone.

"So I thought I better call you," my father said, and he waited for me to say what he should do now.

My mother prayed on her knees at midday, at night, and first thing in the morning. Every day opened up to her to have God's will done in it[11]. Every night she totted up[12] what she'd done and said and thought, to see how it squared with Him[13]. That kind of life is dreary[14], people think, but they're missing the point[15]. For one thing, such a life can never be boring. And nothing can happen to you that you can't make

1 **burden:** peso • 2 **took it hard:** encarou com dificuldade • 3 **willingly:** de bom grado • 4 **couch:** sofá • 5 **she had picked:** ela tinha colhido • 6 **was setting them on the windowsill to ripen:** os tinha colocado no beiral da janela para amadurecer • 7 **went wobbly:** começou a tremer • 8 **meandering:** divagando • 9 **amazement:** estupefação, assombro • 10 **quilt:** colcha • 11 **every day opened up to her to have God's will done in it:** todos os dias começavam para ela com a expectativa de ver cumprida a vontade de Deus • 12 **she totted up:** fazia um balanço • 13 **how it squared with Him:** se estava de acordo com Ele • 14 **dreary:** triste, lúgubre • 15 **they're missing the point:** não entendem

use of. Even if you're wracked[1] by troubles, and sick and poor and ugly, you've got your soul to carry through life like a treasure on a platter[2]. Going upstairs to pray after the noon meal, my mother would be full of energy and expectation, seriously smiling.

She was saved at a camp meeting when she was fourteen. That was the same summer that her own mother—my grandmother—died. For a few years, my mother went to meetings with a lot of other people who'd been saved, some who'd been saved over and over again, enthusiastic old sinners[3]. She could tell stories about what went on[4] at those meetings, the singing and hollering and wildness[5]. She told about one old man getting up and shouting, "Come down, O Lord, come down among us now! Come down through the roof and I'll pay for the shingles[6]!"

She was back to being just an Anglican[7], a serious one, by the time she got married. She was twenty-five then, and my father was thirty-eight. A tall good-looking couple, good dancers, good cardplayers, sociable. But serious people—that's how I would try to describe them. Serious the way hardly anybody[8] is anymore. My father was not religious in the way my mother was. He was an Anglican, an Orangeman[9], a Conservative, because that's what he had been brought up[10] to be. He was the son who got left on

1 **wracked:** atormentado • 2 **platter:** bandeja • 3 **sinners:** pecadores • 4 **what went on:** o que acontecia • 5 **hollering and wildness:** gritaria e chamados desenfreados • 6 **shingles:** telhas • 7 **she was back to being just an Anglican:** voltou a ser uma anglicana normal • 8 **hardly anybody:** quase ninguém • 9 **Orangeman:** protestante da Irlanda do Norte favorável ao Reino Unido • 10 **brought up:** educado

the farm with his parents and took care of them till they died. He met my mother, he waited for her, they married; he thought himself lucky then to have a family to work for. (I have two brothers, and I had a baby sister who died.) I have a feeling that my father never slept with any woman before my mother, and never with her until he married her. And he had to wait, because my mother wouldn't get married until she had paid back to her own father every cent he had spent on her since her mother died. She had kept track of[1] everything—board[2], books, clothes—so that she could pay it back. When she married, she had no nest egg[3], as teachers usually did, no hope chest[4], sheets[5], or dishes. My father used to say, with a sombre, joking face, that he had hoped to get a woman with money in the bank. "But you take the money in the bank, you have to take the face that goes with it," he said, "and sometimes that's no bargain[6]."

The house we lived in had big, high rooms, with dark-green blinds[7] on the windows. When the blinds were pulled down against the sun, I used to like to move my head and catch the light flashing through the holes and cracks[8]. Another thing I liked looking at was chimney stains[9], old or fresh, which I could turn into animals, people's faces, even distant cities. I told my own two boys about that, and their father, Dan Casey, said, "See, your mom's folks were so poor, they couldn't

1 **she had kept track of:** ela tinha anotado tudo • 2 **board:** refeições • 3 **nest egg:** poupança • 4 **hope chest:** enxoval • 5 **sheets:** lençóis • 6 **bargain:** negócio • 7 **blinds:** persianas • 8 **cracks:** fendas • 9 **chimney stains:** manchas de fuligem

afford TV, so they got these stains on the ceiling—your mom had to watch the stains on the ceiling!" He always liked to kid me about thinking poor was anything great[1].

When my father was very old, I figured out[2] that he didn't mind[3] people doing new sorts of things—for instance, my getting divorced—as much as he minded them having new sorts of reasons for doing them.

Thank God he never had to know about the commune[4].

"The Lord never intended[5]," he used to say. Sitting around with the other old men in the Home, in the long, dim porch behind the spirea bushes[6], he talked about how the Lord never intended for people to tear around[7] the country on motorbikes and snowmobiles[8]. And how the Lord never intended for nurses' uniforms to be pants[9]. The nurses didn't mind at all. They called him "Handsome," and told me he was a real old sweetheart, a real old religious gentleman. They marvelled at his thick black hair, which he kept until he died. They washed and combed[10] it beautifully, wet-waved[11] it with their fingers.

Sometimes, with all their care, he was a little unhappy. He wanted to go home. He worried about the cows, the fences[12], about who was getting up to light the fire. A few

1 **he always liked to kid me about thinking poor was anything great:** sempre brincava de me fazer pensar que ser pobre era bom • 2 **I figured out:** me dei conta • 3 **he didn't mind:** não se importava • 4 **commune:** comuna, como a dos *hippies* • 5 **the Lord never intended:** não era a intenção do Senhor • 6 **spirea bushes:** arbustos de grinalda-de-noiva • 7 **to tear around:** atravessar a toda velocidade • 8 **snowmobiles**: motos de neve • 9 **pants:** calças • 10 **combed:** o penteavam • 11 **wet-waved:** ondulavam-no • 12 **fences:** cercas

flashes of meanness[1]—very few. Once, he gave me a sneaky[2], unfriendly look when I went in; he said, "I'm surprised you haven't worn all the skin off your knees[3] by now."

I laughed. I said, "What doing? Scrubbing floors[4]?"

"Praying!" he said, in a voice like spitting[5].

He didn't know who he was talking to.

I don't remember my mother's hair being anything but white. My mother went white in her twenties, and never saved any of her young hair, which had been brown. I used to try to get her to tell what color brown.

"Dark."

"Like Brent, or like Dolly?" Those were two workhorses[6] we had, a team.

"I don't know. It wasn't horsehair."

"Was it like chocolate?"

"Something like."

"Weren't you sad when it went white?"

"No. I was glad."

"Why?"

"I was glad that I wouldn't have hair anymore that was the same color as my father's."

Hatred[7] is always a sin, my mother told me. Remember that. One drop[8] of hatred in your soul[9] will spread[10] and discolor everything like a drop of black ink[11] in white milk.

1 **meanness:** maldade • 2 **sneaky:** furtivo • 3 **you haven't worn all the skin off your knees:** não tenha ralado os joelhos • 4 **scrubbing floors:** esfregando o chão • 5 **like spitting:** como que cuspindo • 6 **workhorses:** cavalos de carga • 7 **hatred:** ódio • 8 **drop:** gota • 9 **soul:** alma • 10 **will spread:** vai se espalhar • 11 **ink:** tinta

I was struck by that[1] and meant to try it, but knew I shouldn't waste[2] the milk.

All these things I remember. All the things I know, or have been told, about people I never even saw. I was named Euphemia, after my mother's mother. A terrible name, such as nobody has nowadays. At home they called me Phemie, but when I started to work, I called myself Fame. My husband, Dan Casey, called me Fame. Then in the bar of the Shamrock Hotel, years later, after my divorce, when I was going out[3], a man said to me, "Fame, I've been meaning to ask you[4], just what is it you are famous for?"

"I don't know," I told him. "I don't know, unless it's for wasting my time talking to jerks[5] like you."

After that I thought of changing it altogether, to something like Joan, but unless I moved away from here, how could I do that?

In the summer of 1947, when I was twelve, I helped my mother paper[6] the downstairs bedroom, the spare room[7]. My mother's sister, Beryl, was coming to visit us. These two sisters hadn't seen each other for years. Very soon after their mother died, their father married again. He went to live in Minneapolis, then in Seattle, with his new wife and his younger daughter, Beryl. My mother wouldn't go with

1 **I was struck by that:** isso me impressionou • 2 **waste:** desperdiçar • 3 **when I was going out:** quando saía • 4 **I've been meaning to ask:** queria perguntar • 5 **jerks:** idiotas • 6 **paper:** colocar papel de parede • 7 **the spare room:** o quarto de hóspedes

them. She stayed on in the town of Ramsay, where they had been living. She was boarded with a childless couple[1] who had been neighbors. She and Beryl had met only once or twice since they were grown up. Beryl lived in California.

The paper had a design of cornflowers on a white ground. My mother had got it at a reduced price, because it was the end of a lot[2]. This meant we had trouble matching the pattern[3], and behind the door we had to do some tricky fitting with scraps and strips[4]. This was before the days of pre-pasted wallpaper[5]. We had a trestle table[6] set up in the front room, and we mixed the paste and swept it[7] onto the back of the paper with wide brushes[8], watching for lumps[9]. We worked with the windows up, screens[10] fitted under them, the front door open, the screen door closed. The country we could see through the mesh[11] of screens and the wavery[12] old window glass was all hot and flowering—milkweed[13] and wild carrot in the pastures, mustard rampaging in the clover[14], some fields creamy[15] with the buckwheat[16] people grew then. My mother sang. She sang a song she said her own mother used to sing when she and Beryl were little girls.

1 **she was boarded with a childless couple**: foi hospedada por um casal sem filhos • 2 **the end of a lot:** o final do lote • 3 **we had trouble matching the pattern:** tivemos problemas para manter a continuidade da estampa • 4 **we had to do some tricky fitting with scraps and strips:** tivemos que encaixar com remendos • 5 **pre-pasted wallpaper:** papel com camada adesiva • 6 **trestle table:** mesa sobre cavaletes • 7 **swept it:** o estendíamos • 8 **brushes:** pincéis; brochas • 9 **lumps:** protuberâncias • 10 **screens:** telas • 11 **mesh:** malha • 12 **wavery:** ondulado • 13 **milkweed:** serralha-branca • 14 **mustard rampaging in the clover:** mostarda brotando no meio dos trevos • 15 **creamy:** cor de creme • 16 **buckwheat**: trigo sarraceno

"I once had a sweetheart[1]*, but now I have none.*
He's gone and he's left me to weep and to moan[2]*.*
He's gone and he's left me, but contented I'll be,
For I'll get another one, better than he!"

I was excited because Beryl was coming, a visitor, all the way from California. Also because I had gone to town in late June to write the Entrance Examinations, and was hoping to hear soon that I had passed with honors[3]. Everybody who had finished Grade 8[4] in the country schools had to go into town to write those examinations. I loved that—the rustling sheets of foolscap[5], the important silence, the big stone high-school building, all the old initials carved[6] in the desks, darkened with varnish. The first burst[7] of summer outside, the green and yellow light, the townlike chestnut trees[8], and honeysuckle[9]. And all it was was this same town, where I have lived now more than half my life. I wondered at it[10]. And at myself, drawing maps with ease and solving problems, knowing quantities of answers. I thought I was so clever. But I wasn't clever enough to understand the simplest thing. I didn't even understand that examinations made no difference in my case. I wouldn't be going to high school. How could I? That was before there were school buses; you had to board in town. My parents didn't have the money.

1 **sweetheart**: namorado • 2 **he's left me to weep and to moan**: me deixou chorando e gemendo • 3 **I had passed with honors:** passei com louvor • 4 **Grade 8**: último ano antes do ensino médio (13-14 anos) • 5 **the rustling sheets of foolscap:** o farfalhar do papel almaço • 6 **carved**: gravadas • 7 **burst:** explosão • 8 **the townlike chestnut trees:** as castanheiras típicas da cidade • 9 **honeysuckle:** madressilva • 10 **I wondered at it:** fiquei maravilhada

They operated on very little cash, as many farmers[1] did then. The payments from the cheese factory were about all that came in regularly. And they didn't think of my life going in that direction, the high-school direction. They thought that I would stay at home and help my mother, maybe hire out to help women[2] in the neighborhood who were sick or having a baby. Until such time as I got married. That was what they were waiting to tell me when I got the results of the examinations.

You would think my mother might have a different idea, since she had been a schoolteacher herself. But she said God didn't care. God isn't interested in what kind of job or what kind of education anybody has, she told me. He doesn't care two hoots[3] about that, and it's what He cares about that matters[4].

This was the first time I understood how God could become a real opponent, not just some kind of nuisance[5] or large decoration.

My mother's name as a child was Marietta. That continued to be her name, of course, but until Beryl came I never heard her called by it. My father always said Mother. I had a childish notion—I knew it was childish—that Mother suited[6] my mother better than it did other mothers. Mother, not Mama. When I was away from her, I could not think what my mother's face was like, and this frightened me. Sitting in

1 **farmers:** fazendeiros • 2 **hire out to help women:** sair para ajudar mulheres • 3 **he doesn't care two hoots:** não estava nem aí • 4 **that matters:** o que importa • 5 **nuisance:** um estorvo • 6 **suited:** ficava melhor para, combinava

school, just over a hill from home, I would try to picture[1] my mother's face. Sometimes I thought that if I couldn't do it, that might mean my mother was dead. But I had a sense of her all the time, and would be reminded of her by the most unlikely[2] things—an upright piano[3], or a tall white loaf of bread[4]. That's ridiculous, but true.

Marietta, in my mind, was separate, not swallowed up in my mother's grownup body[5]. Marietta was still running around loose[6] up in her town of Ramsay, on the Ottawa River. In that town, the streets were full of horses and puddles[7], and darkened by men who came in from the bush[8] on weekends. Loggers[9]. There were eleven hotels on the main street, where the loggers stayed, and drank.

The house Marietta lived in was halfway up a steep street[10] climbing from the river. It was a double house, with two bay windows[11] in front, and a wooden trellis[12] that separated the two front porches. In the other half of the house lived the Sutcliffes, the people Marietta was to board with[13] after her mother died and her father left town. Mr. Sutcliffe was an Englishman, a telegraph operator. His wife was German. She always made coffee instead of tea. She made strudel. The dough[14] for the strudel hung down over the edges of the table like a fine cloth. It sometimes looked to Marietta like a skin.

1 **to picture:** imaginar • 2 **unlikely:** improváveis • 3 **an upright piano:** piano vertical • 4 **loaf of bread:** um filão de pão • 5 **not swallowed up in my mother's grownup body:** não integrada ao corpo adulto da minha mãe • 6 **Marietta was still running around loose:** Marietta ainda corria solta por aí • 7 **puddles:** poças • 8 **the bush:** bosque • 9 **loggers:** lenhadores • 10 **halfway up a steep street:** na metade da subida de uma rua inclinada • 11 **bay windows:** janelas de sacada • 12 **wooden trellis:** treliça de madeira • 13 **to board with:** com quem iria morar • 14 **dough:** massa

Mrs. Sutcliffe was the one who talked Marietta's mother out of hanging herself[1].

Marietta was home from school that day, because it was Saturday. She woke up late and heard the silence in the house. She was always scared of that—a silent house—and as soon as she opened the door after school she would call, "Mama! Mama!" Often her mother wouldn't answer. But she would be there. Marietta would hear with relief the rattle of the stove grate[2] or the steady slap of the iron[3].

That morning, she didn't hear anything. She came downstairs, and got herself a slice of bread and butter and molasses[4], folded over[5]. She opened the cellar door and called. She went into the front room and peered[6] out the window, through the bridal fern[7]. She saw her little sister, Beryl, and some other neighborhood children rolling down the bit of grassy terrace to the sidewalk[8], picking themselves up[9] and scrambling[10] to the top and rolling down again.

"Mama?" called Marietta. She walked through the house to the back yard[11]. It was late spring, the day was cloudy and mild[12]. In the sprouting[13] vegetable gardens, the earth was damp[14], and the leaves on the trees seemed suddenly

1 **the one who talked Marietta's mother out of hanging herself:** aquela que convenceu a mãe de Marietta a não se enforcar • 2 **the rattle of the stove grate:** barulho contínuo da fornalha do fogão • 3 **the steady slap of the iron:** a batida constante do ferro de passar • 4 **molasses:** melaço • 5 **folded over:** dobrado • 6 **peered:** olhou detidamente • 7 **bridal fern:** samambaia (em forma de buquê de noiva) • 8 **rolling down the bit of grassy terrace to the sidewalk:** rolando abaixo desde o terreno gramado até a calçada • 9 **picking themselves up:** levantando-se • 10 **scrambling:** subindo afoitos • 11 **back yard:** quintal dos fundos • 12 **mild:** brando • 13 **sprouting:** brotando • 14 **damp:** úmida

full-sized[1], letting down drops of water left over from the rain of the night before.

"Mama?" calls Marietta under the trees, under the clothesline[2].

At the end of the yard is a small barn[3], where they keep firewood, and some tools and old furniture. A chair, a straight-backed[4] wooden chair, can be seen through the open doorway. On the chair, Marietta sees her mother's feet, her mother's black laced shoes[5]. Then the long, printed[6] cotton summer work dress, the apron[7], the rolled-up sleeves[8]. Her mother's shiny-looking white arms, and neck, and face.

Her mother stood on the chair and didn't answer. She didn't look at Marietta, but smiled and tapped her foot[9], as if to say, "Here I am, then. What are you going to do about it?" Something looked wrong about her, beyond the fact that she was standing on a chair and smiling in this queer, tight way[10]. Standing on an old chair with back rungs missing[11], which she had pulled out to the middle of the barn floor, where it teetered on the bumpy earth[12]. There was a shadow on her neck.

The shadow was a rope, a noose on the end of a rope that hung down from a beam overhead[13].

1 **full-sized:** de tamanho normal • 2 **clothesline:** varal • 3 **barn:** celeiro • 4 **straight-backed:** de encosto reto • 5 **laced shoes:** sapatos de cadarço • 6 **printed:** estampado • 7 **apron:** avental • 8 **rolled-up sleeves:** mangas arregaçadas • 9 **tapped her foot:** batia com o pé • 10 **in this queer, tight way:** desse jeito estranho e tenso • 11 **with back rungs missing:** no encosto da qual faltavam barrotes • 12 **it teetered on the bumpy earth:** onde oscilava sobre o chão acidentado • 13 **a noose on the end of a rope that hung down from a beam overhead:** um nó no final da corda pendurada de uma viga

"Mama?" says Marietta, in a fainter[1] voice. "Mama. Come down, please." Her voice is faint because she fears that any yell or cry[2] might jolt her mother into movement[3], cause her to step off the chair and throw her weight on the rope[4]. But even if Marietta wanted to yell she couldn't. Nothing but this pitiful thread of a voice[5] is left to her—just as in a dream when a beast or a machine is bearing down on you[6].

"Go and get your father."

That was what her mother told her to do, and Marietta obeyed. With terror in her legs, she ran. In her nightgown[7], in the middle of a Saturday morning, she ran. She ran past Beryl and the other children, still tumbling down the slope[8]. She ran along the sidewalk, which was at that time a boardwalk[9], then on the unpaved[10] street, full of last night's puddles. The street crossed the railway tracks[11]. At the foot of the hill, it intersected the main street of the town. Between the main street and the river were some warehouses[12] and the buildings of small manufacturers. That was where Marietta's father had his carriage works[13]. Wagons[14], buggies[15], sleds[16] were made there. In fact, Marietta's father had invented a new sort of sled to carry logs in the bush[17]. It had

1 **fainter:** mais fraca • 2 **any yell or cry:** qualquer grito ou choro • 3 **might jolt her mother into movement:** pudesse provocar um movimento de sua mãe • 4 **throw her weight on the rope:** jogar seu peso na corda • 5 **pitiful thread of a voice:** lamentável filete de voz • 6 **bearing down on you:** joga-se sobre você • 7 **nightgown:** camisola • 8 **tumbling down the slope:** rolando ladeira abaixo • 9 **boardwalk:** deque de tábuas • 10 **unpaved:** sem asfalto • 11 **railway tracks:** trilhos de trem • 12 **warehouses:** armazéns • 13 **carriage works:** fábrica de carruagens • 14 **wagons:** carros de animais • 15 **buggies:** carroças • 16 **sleds:** trenós • 17 **to carry logs in the bush:** para carregar troncos no bosque

been patented. He was just getting started in Ramsay. (Later on, in the States, he made money. A man fond of[1] hotel bars, barbershops, harness races[2], women, but not afraid of work —give him credit[3].)

Marietta did not find him at work that day. The office was empty. She ran out into the yard where the men were working. She stumbled[4] in the fresh sawdust[5]. The men laughed and shook their heads[6] at her. No. Not here. Not a-here right now. No. Why don't you try upstreet? Wait. Wait a minute. Hadn't you better get some clothes on first[7]?

They didn't mean any harm[8]. They didn't have the sense[9] to see that something must be wrong. But Marietta never could stand[10] men laughing. There were always places she hated to go past, let alone into[11], and that was the reason. Men laughing. Because of that, she hated barbershops, hated their smell. (When she started going to dances later on with my father, she asked him not to put any dressing[12] on his hair, because the smell reminded her.) A bunch[13] of men standing out on the street, outside a hotel, seemed to Marietta like a clot of poison[14]. You tried not to hear what they were saying, but you could be sure it was vile. If they didn't say anything, they laughed and vileness spread out from

1 **fond of:** apreciador • 2 **harness races:** corridas de trote • 3 **give him credit:** é preciso reconhecer • 4 **she stumbled:** tropeçou • 5 **sawdust:** serragem • 6 **shook their heads:** acenaram negativamente com a cabeça • 7 **hadn't you better get some clothes on first?:** não seria melhor se vestir primeiro? • 8 **they didn't mean any harm:** não tinham má intenção • 9 **the sense:** a noção • 10 **never could stand:** nunca suportou • 11 **let alone into:** muito menos entrar • 12 **dressing:** brilhantina • 13 **a bunch:** um grupo • 14 **a clot of poison:** concentrado de veneno

them—poison—just the same. It was only after Marietta was saved that she could walk right past them. Armed by God, she walked through their midst[1] and nothing stuck[2] to her, nothing scorched[3] her; she was safe as Daniel.

Now she turned and ran, straight back the way she had come. Up the hill, running to get home. She thought she had made a mistake leaving her mother. Why did her mother tell her to go? Why did she want her father? Quite possibly so that she could greet him[4] with the sight[5] of her own warm body swinging[6] on the end of a rope. Marietta should have stayed—she should have stayed and talked her mother out of it. She should have run to Mrs. Sutcliffe, or any neighbor, not wasted time this way. She hadn't thought who could help, who could even believe what she was talking about. She had the idea that all families except her own lived in peace, that threats[7] and miseries didn't exist in other people's houses, and couldn't be explained there.

A train was coming into town. Marietta had to wait. Passengers looked out at her from its windows. She broke out wailing[8] in the faces of those strangers. When the train passed, she continued up the hill—a spectacle, with her hair uncombed[9], her feet bare[10] and muddy[11], in her nightgown, with a wild, wet face. By the time she ran into her own yard, in sight of the barn, she was howling[12]. "Mama!" she was howling. "Mama!"

1 **through their midst:** no meio deles • 2 **stuck:** grudava nela • 3 **scorched her:** a queimava • 4 **she could greet him:** podia recebê-lo • 5 **sight:** visão, imagem • 6 **swinging:** balançando • 7 **threats:** ameaças • 8 **she broke out wailing:** desatou a chorar desconsolada • 9 **uncombed:** despenteado • 10 **bare:** descalços • 11 **muddy:** cheios de barro • 12 **howling:** urrando

Nobody was there. The chair was standing just where it had been before. The rope was dangling over the back of it[1]. Marietta was sure that her mother had gone ahead and done it[2]. Her mother was already dead—she had been cut down and taken away.

But warm, fat hands settled down[3] on her shoulders[4], and Mrs. Sutcliffe said, "Marietta. Stop the noise. Marietta. Child. Stop the crying. Come inside. She is well, Marietta. Come inside and you will see."

Mrs. Sutcliffe's foreign voice said, "Mari-et-cha," giving the name a rich, important sound. She was as kind as could be[5]. When Marietta lived with the Sutcliffes later, she was treated as the daughter of the household[6], and it was a household just as peaceful and comfortable as she had imagined other households to be. But she never felt like a daughter there.

In Mrs. Sutcliffe's kitchen, Beryl sat on the floor eating a raisin cookie[7] and playing with the black-and-white cat, whose name was Dickie. Marietta's mother sat at the table, with a cup of coffee in front of her.

"She was silly," Mrs. Sutcliffe said. Did she mean Marietta's mother or Marietta herself? She didn't have many English words to describe things.

Marietta's mother laughed, and Marietta blacked out[8]. She fainted[9], after running all that way uphill, howling, in the

1 **was dangling over the back of it:** estava balançando pendurada atrás da cadeira • 2 **had gone ahead and done it:** tinha ido em frente e feito aquilo • 3 **settled down:** acomodaram-se • 4 **shoulders:** ombros • 5 **she was as kind as could be:** era tão amável quanto podia • 6 **household:** da casa, do lar • 7 **raisin cookie:** bolacha de uva-passa • 8 **blacked out:** "apagou" • 9 **she fainted:** desmaiou

warm, damp morning. Next thing she knew[1], she was taking black, sweet coffee from a spoon held by Mrs. Sutcliffe. Beryl picked Dickie up by the front legs and offered him as a cheering[2] present. Marietta's mother was still sitting at the table.

Her heart was broken. That was what I always heard my mother say. That was the end of it. Those words lifted up the story[3] and sealed it shut[4]. I never asked, Who broke it? I never asked. What was the men's poison talk? What was the meaning of the word "vile"?

Marietta's mother laughed after not hanging herself. She sat at Mrs. Sutcliffe's kitchen table long ago and laughed. Her heart was broken.

I always had a feeling, with my mother's talk and stories, of something swelling out behind[5]. Like a cloud you couldn't see through, or get to the end of. There was a cloud, a poison, that had touched my mother's life. And when I grieved my mother[6], I became part of it. Then I would beat my head against[7] my mother's stomach and breasts, against her tall, firm front, demanding to be forgiven[8]. My mother would tell me to ask God. But it wasn't God, it was my mother I had to get straight with[9]. It seemed as if she knew something

1 **next thing she knew:** quando voltou a si • 2 **cheering:** reconfortante • 3 **lifted up the story:** faziam a história chegar ao seu ápice • 4 **sealed it shut:** a davam por encerrada • 5 **something swelling out behind:** alguma coisa se agigantando por trás de tudo • 6 **I grieved my mother:** chorei pela minha mãe • 7 **I would beat my head against:** batia a cabeça contra • 8 **demanding to be forgiven:** clamando seu perdão • 9 **I had to get straight with:** com quem tinha que deixar as coisas claras

about me that was worse, far worse, than ordinary lies and tricks and meanness[1]; it was a really sickening shame[2]. I beat against my mother's front to make her forget that.

My brothers weren't bothered by any of this[3]. I don't think so. They seemed to me like cheerful savages[4], running around free, not having to learn much. And when I just had the two boys myself, no daughters, I felt as if something could stop now—the stories, and griefs[5], the old puzzles you can't resist or solve.

Aunt Beryl said not to call her Aunt. "I'm not used to being anybody's aunt, honey. I'm not even anybody's momma. I'm just me. Call me Beryl."

Beryl had started out as a stenographer[6], and now she had her own typing and bookkeeping business[7], which employed many girls. She had arrived with a man friend, whose name was Mr. Florence. Her letter had said that she would be getting a ride with a friend[8], but she hadn't said whether the friend would be staying or going on[9]. She hadn't even said if it was a man or a woman.

Mr. Florence was staying. He was a tall, thin man with a long, tanned[10] face, very light-colored eyes, and a way of twitching[11] the corner of his mouth that might have been a smile.

1 **ordinary lies and tricks and meanness:** mentiras comuns, artimanhas e maldade • 2 **a really sickening shame:** uma vergonha repulsiva • 3 **weren't bothered by any of this:** não se preocupavam com nada disso • 4 **cheerful savages:** selvagens alegres • 5 **griefs:** pesares • 6 **stenographer:** taquígrafa • 7 **bookkeeping business:** negócio de contabilidade • 8 **she would be getting a ride with a friend:** vinha de carona com um amigo • 9 **going on:** estava de passagem • 10 **tanned:** bronzeada • 11 **twitching:** torcer o canto da boca

He was the one who got to sleep in the room that my mother and I had papered, because he was the stranger, and a man. Beryl had to sleep with me. At first we thought that Mr. Florence was quite rude[1], because he wasn't used to our way of talking and we weren't used to his. The first morning, my father said to Mr. Florence, "Well, I hope you got some kind of a sleep[2] on that old bed in there." (The spare-room bed was heavenly[3], with a feather tick[4].) This was Mr. Florence's cue to say[5] that he had never slept better.

Mr. Florence twitched. He said, "I slept on worse."

His favorite place to be was in his car. His car was a royal-blue Chrysler, from the first batch turned out[6] after the war. Inside it, the upholstery[7] and floor covering[8] and roof and door padding[9] were all pearl gray. Mr. Florence kept the names of those colors in mind[10] and corrected you if you said just "blue" or "gray."

"Mouse skin is what it looks like to me," said Beryl rambunctiously[11]. "I tell him it's just mouse skin!"

The car was parked at the side of the house, under the locust trees[12]. Mr. Florence sat inside with the windows rolled up[13], smoking, in the rich new-car smell.

1 **rude:** mal-educado • 2 **I hope you got some kind of a sleep:** espero que tenha dormido um pouco • 3 **heavenly:** divino • 4 **feather tick:** colchão de plumas • 5 **Mr. Florence's cue to say:** a "deixa" do sr. Florence para dizer • 6 **the first batch turned out:** a primeira leva produzida • 7 **upholstery:** tapeçaria • 8 **covering:** revestimento • 9 **padding:** acolchoado • 10 **kept the names of those colours in mind:** guardava na memória os nomes dessas cores • 11 **rambunctiously:** com rebeldia • 12 **locust trees:** acácia-falsa • 13 **rolled up:** levantadas

"I'm afraid[1] we're not doing much to entertain your friend," my mother said.

"I wouldn't worry[2] about him," said Beryl. She always spoke about Mr. Florence as if there was a joke about him that only she appreciated. I wondered long afterward[3] if he had a bottle in the glove compartment[4] and took a nip[5] from time to time to keep his spirits up[6]. He kept his hat on.

Beryl herself was being entertained enough for two. Instead of staying in the house and talking to my mother, as a lady visitor usually did, she demanded to be shown everything there was to see on a farm. She said that I was to take her around and explain things, and see that she didn't fall into any manure piles[7].

I didn't know what to show. I took Beryl to the icehouse, where chunks[8] of ice the size of dresser drawers[9], or bigger, lay buried in sawdust[10]. Every few days, my father would chop off[11] a piece of ice and carry it to the kitchen, where it melted[12] in a tin-lined box[13] and cooled the milk and butter.

Beryl said she had never had any idea ice came in pieces that big. She seemed intent on finding[14] things strange, or horrible, or funny.

1 **I'm afraid:** temo que • 2 **I wouldn't worry:** não me preocuparia • 3 **I wondered long afterward:** muito tempo depois me perguntei • 4 **glove compartment:** porta-luvas • 5 **took a nip:** tomava um gole • 6 **to keep his spirits up:** para se animar • 7 **manure piles:** montes de esterco; adubo • 8 **chunks:** pedaços • 9 **dresser drawers:** gavetas de penteadeira • 10 **lay buried in sawdust:** estavam enterrados na serragem • 11 **would chop off:** cortava • 12 **it melted:** derretia • 13 **tin-lined box:** caixa de latão • 14 **she seemed intent on finding:** parecia empenhada em encontrar

"Where in the world do you get ice that big?"

I couldn't tell if that was a joke.

"Off of the lake[1]," I said.

"Off of the lake! Do you have lakes up here that have ice on them all summer?"

I told her how my father cut the ice on the lake every winter and hauled it home[2], and buried it in sawdust, and that kept it from melting[3].

Beryl said, "That's amazing!"

"Well, it melts a little," I said. I was deeply disappointed in Beryl.

"That's really amazing."

Beryl went along[4] when I went to get the cows. A scarecrow in white slacks[5] (this was what my father called her afterward), with a white sun hat tied under her chin[6] by a flaunting red ribbon[7]. Her fingernails and toenails—she wore sandals—were painted to match[8] the ribbon. She wore the small, dark sunglasses people wore at that time. (Not the people I knew—they didn't own sunglasses.) She had a big red mouth, a loud laugh, hair of an unnatural color and a high gloss[9], like cherry wood. She was so noisy and shiny, so glamorously got up[10], that it was hard to tell whether she was good-looking, or happy, or anything.

1 **off of the lake**: do lago • 2 **hauled it home**: o arrastava até a casa • 3 **kept it from melting:** não o deixava derreter • 4 **went along:** me acompanhou • 5 **a scarecrow in white slacks:** um espantalho de calça branca • 6 **tied under her chin:** amarrado embaixo do queixo • 7 **by a flaunting red ribbon:** com uma fita vermelha espalhafatosa • 8 **to match:** para combinar • 9 **a high gloss:** um brilho exagerado • 10 **got up:** arrumada

We didn't have any conversation along the cowpath[1], because Beryl kept her distance from the cows and was busy watching where she stepped[2]. Once I had them all tied in their stalls[3], she came closer. She lit a cigarette. Nobody smoked in the barn. My father and other farmers chewed[4] tobacco there instead. I didn't see how I could ask Beryl to chew tobacco.

"Can you get the milk out of them or does your father have to?" Beryl said. "Is it hard to do?"

I pulled some milk down through the cow's teat. One of the barn cats came over and waited. I shot a thin stream into its mouth[5]. The cat and I were both showing off[6].

"Doesn't that hurt?" said Beryl. "Think if it was you."

I had never thought of a cow's teat as corresponding to any part of myself, and was shaken[7] by this indecency. In fact, I could never grasp[8] a warm, warty[9] teat in such a firm and casual way again.

Beryl slept in a peach-colored rayon nightgown trimmed with écru lace[10]. She had a robe to match[11]. She was just as careful about the word "écru" as Mr. Florence was about his royal blue and pearl gray.

I managed to get undressed and put on my nightgown without any part of me being exposed at any time. An awk-

1 **cowpath:** caminho de vaca • 2 **watching where she stepped:** olhando onde pisava • 3 **stalls:** estábulos • 4 **chewed:** mascavam • 5 **I shot a thin stream into its mouth:** joguei um fino jato na sua boca • 6 **showing off:** exibindo-nos • 7 **shaken:** perturbada • 8 **I could never grasp:** nunca pude agarrar • 9 **warty:** verrugosa • 10 **trimmed with écru lace:** bordada com debrum cru • 11 **she had a robe to match:** tinha um robe combinando

ward business[1]. I left my underpants[2] on, and hoped that Beryl had done the same. The idea of sharing my bed with a grownup[3] was a torment to me. But I did get to see the contents of what Beryl called her beauty kit. Hand-painted glass jars[4] contained puffs of cotton wool[5], talcum powder, milky lotion, ice-blue astringent. Little pots[6] of red and mauve rouge[7]—rather greasy-looking[8]. Blue and black pencils. Emery boards[9], a pumice stone[10], nail polish[11] with an overpowering[12] smell of bananas, face powder in a celluloid box shaped like a shell[13], with the name of a dessert—Apricot Delight[14].

I had heated[15] some water on the coal-oil stove[16] we used in summertime. Beryl scrubbed[17] her face clean, and there was such a change that I almost expected to see makeup lying in strips[18] in the washbowl[19], like the old wallpaper we had soaked[20] and peeled[21]. Beryl's skin was pale now, covered with fine cracks, rather like[22] the shiny mud[23] at the bottom of puddles drying up in early summer.

"Look what happened to my skin," she said. "Dieting. I weighed a hundred and sixty-nine pounds[24] once, I took

1 **an awkward business:** um negócio bizarro • 2 **underpants:** roupa de baixo • 3 **grownup:** adulto • 4 **glass jars:** frascos de vidro • 5 **puffs of cotton wool:** tufos de algodão • 6 **pots:** potes • 7 **mauve rouge:** *blush* cor malva • 8 **rather greasy-looking:** de aspecto bastante gorduroso • 9 **emery boards:** lixas de unha • 10 **a pumice stone:** uma pedra-pomes • 11 **nail polish:** esmalte • 12 **overpowering:** muito forte • 13 **shell:** concha • 14 **Apricot Delight:** delícia de damasco • 15 **I had heated:** havia esquentado • 16 **coal-oil stove:** forno a carvão • 17 **scrubbed:** limpou o rosto esfregando • 18 **makeup lying in strips:** tiras de maquiagem • 19 **washbowl:** bacia • 20 **we had soaked:** tínhamos molhado • 21 **peeled:** descascado • 22 **rather like:** bastante parecido com • 23 **mud:** barro • 24 **a hundred and sixty-nine pounds:** 77 quilos

it off[1] too fast and my face fell in on me[2]. Now I've got this cream, though. It's made from a secret formula and you can't even buy it commercially. Smell it. See, it doesn't smell all perfumy. It smells serious."

She was patting[3] the cream on her face with puffs of cotton wool, patting away until there was nothing to be seen on the surface.

"It smells like lard[4]," I said.

"Christ Almighty[5], I hope I haven't been paying that kind of money to rub[6] lard on my face. Don't tell your mother I swear[7]."

She poured clean water into the drinking glass and wet her comb, then combed her hair wet and twisted each strand round her finger[8], clamping[9] the twisted strand to her head with two crossed pins[10]. I would be doing the same myself, a couple of years later.

"Always do your hair wet[11], else it's no good doing it up at all[12]," Beryl said. "And always roll it under even if you want it to flip up[13]. See?"

When I was doing my hair up—as I did for years—I sometimes thought of this, and thought that of all the pieces of advice people had given me, this was the one I had followed most carefully.

1 **I took it off:** eu os perdi • 2 **fell in on me:** desabou • 3 **patting:** aplicando com batidinhas • 4 **lard:** banha • 5 **Christ Almighty:** Santo Deus • 6 **to rub:** esfregar • 7 **I swear:** falo palavrão • 8 **twisted each strand round her finger:** enroscava cada mecha ao redor do dedo • 9 **clamping:** prendendo • 10 **crossed pins:** grampos cruzados • 11 **do your hair wet:** arrume o cabelo enquanto estiver molhado • 12 **else it's no good doing it up at all:** senão, nem vale a pena arrumar • 13 **roll it under even if you want to flip it up:** enrole o cabelo para dentro mesmo que queira que fique para fora

We put the lamp out[1] and got into bed, and Beryl said, "I never knew it could get so dark. I've never known a dark that was as dark as this." She was whispering[2]. I was slow to understand that she was comparing country nights to city nights, and I wondered if the darkness in Netterfield County could really be greater than that in California.

"Honey?" whispered Beryl. "Are there any animals outside?"

"Cows," I said.

"Yes, but wild animals? Are there bears?"

"Yes," I said. My father had once found bear tracks and droppings in the bush[3], and the apples had all been torn off a wild apple tree[4]. That was years ago, when he was a young man.

Beryl moaned and giggled[5]. "Think if Mr. Florence had to go out in the night and he ran into[6] a bear!"

Next day was Sunday. Beryl and Mr. Florence drove my brothers and me to Sunday school[7] in the Chrysler. That was at ten o'clock in the morning. They came back at eleven to bring my parents to church.

"Hop in[8]," Beryl said to me. "You too," she said to the boys. "We're going for a drive[9]."

1 **we put the lamp out:** apagamos a lâmpada • 2 **whispering:** sussurrando • 3 **bear tracks and droppings in the bush**: pegadas e excrementos de urso no bosque • 4 **torn off a wild apple tree:** arrancadas de uma macieira silvestre • 5 **moaned and giggled:** gemeu e deu uma risadinha • 6 **he ran into:** se encontrasse; desse de cara • 7 **Sunday school:** escola dominical • 8 **hop in:** suba • 9 **we're going for a drive:** vamos dar uma volta (de carro)

Beryl was dressed up in a satiny ivory dress with red dots[1], and a red-lined frill over the hips[2], and red high-heeled[3] shoes. Mr. Florence wore a pale-blue summer suit[4].

"Aren't you going to church?" I said. That was what people dressed up for, in my experience.

Beryl laughed. "Honey, this isn't Mr. Florence's kind of religion."

I was used to going straight from Sunday school into church, and sitting for another hour and a half. In summer, the open windows let in the cedary smell of the graveyard[5] and the occasional, almost sacrilegious sound of a car swooshing by[6] on the road. Today we spent this time driving through country I had never seen before. I had never seen it, though it was less than twenty miles[7] from home. Our truck went to the cheese factory, to church, and to town on Saturday nights. The nearest thing to[8] a drive was when it went to the dump[9]. I had seen the near end of Bell's Lake, because that was where my father cut the ice in winter. You couldn't get close to it in summer; the shoreline was all choked up with bulrushes[10]. I had thought that the other end of the lake would look pretty much the same, but when we drove there today, I saw cottages[11], docks[12] and boats, dark water reflecting

1 **a satiny ivory dress with red dots:** um vestido de cetim marfim com bolinhas vermelhas • 2 **a red-lined frill over the hips:** um babado vermelho na altura do quadril • 3 **high-heeled:** sapato de salto alto • 4 **suit:** traje • 5 **let in the cedary smell of the graveyard:** deixavam entrar o perfume de cedro do cemitério • 6 **swooshing by:** que passava em disparada • 7 **twenty miles:** 32 quilômetros • 8 **the nearest thing to:** o mais parecido com • 9 **dump:** depósito de lixo • 10 **the shoreline was all choked up with bulrushes:** a costa estava obstruída por juncos • 11 **cottages:** cabanas; chalés • 12 **docks:** docas

the trees. All this and I hadn't known about it. This, too, was Bell's Lake. I was glad to have seen it at last, but in some way not altogether glad[1] of the surprise.

Finally, a white frame building[2] appeared, with verandas[3] and potted flowers[4], and some twinkling poplar trees[5] in front. The Wildwood Inn. Today the same building is covered with stucco and done up[6] with Tudor beams and called the Hideaway[7]. The poplar trees have been cut down for a parking lot.

On the way back[8] to the church to pick up[9] my parents, Mr. Florence turned in to the farm next to ours[10], which belonged[11] to the McAllisters. The McAllisters were Catholics. Our two families were neighborly but not close[12].

"Come on, boys, out you get[13]," said Beryl to my brothers. "Not you," she said to me. "You stay put[14]." She herded[15] the little boys up to the porch, where some McAllisters were watching. They were in their raggedy[16] home clothes, because their church, or Mass[17], or whatever it was[18], got out early[19]. Mrs. McAllister came out and stood listening, rather dumbfounded[20], to Beryl's laughing talk.

1 **not altogether glad:** não totalmente satisfeita • 2 **a white frame building:** construção branca de madeira • 3 **veranda:** varanda; pórticos • 4 **potted flowers:** vasos de flores • 5 **twinkling poplar trees:** álamos que brilhavam • 6 **done up:** renovado • 7 **the Hideaway:** o Refúgio • 8 **on the way back:** no caminho de volta • 9 **to pick up:** buscar • 10 **turned in to the farm next to ours:** virou para entrar na fazenda vizinha à nossa • 11 **belonged:** pertencia • 12 **neighborly but not close:** bons vizinhos, mas não próximos • 13 **come on, boys, out you get:** vamos, meninos, para fora • 14 **you stay put:** não se mexa • 15 **she herded:** ela arrebanhou • 16 **raggedy:** esfarrapadas • 17 **Mass:** missa • 18 **or whatever it was:** o que quer que fosse • 19 **got out early:** acabava cedo • 20 **dumbfounded:** estupefata

Beryl came back to the car by herself. "There," she said. "They're going to play with the neighbor children."

Play with McAllisters? Besides[1] being Catholics, all but the baby were girls.

"They've still got their good clothes on," I said.

"So what? Can't they have a good time with their good clothes on? I do!"

My parents were taken by surprise as well[2]. Beryl got out[3] and told my father he was to ride in the front seat, for the legroom[4]. She got into the back, with my mother and me. Mr. Florence turned again onto the Bell's Lake road, and Beryl announced that we were all going to the Wildwood Inn for dinner.

"You're all dressed up[5], why not take advantage[6]?" she said. "We dropped the boys off with your neighbors[7]. I thought they might be too young to appreciate it. The neighbors were happy to have them." She said with a further emphasis that it was to be their treat[8]. Hers and Mr. Florence's.

"Well, now," said my father. He probably didn't have five dollars in his pocket. "Well, now. I wonder do they let the farmers in?"

He made various jokes along this line[9]. In the hotel dining room, which was all in white—white tablecloths[10], white

1 **besides:** além de • 2 **were taken by surprise as well:** também foram pegos de surpresa • 3 **got out:** saiu • 4 **legroom:** espaço para as pernas • 5 **dressed up:** bem vestidos • 6 **take advantage:** aproveitar • 7 **we dropped the boys off with your neighbors:** deixamos os meninos com os vizinhos • 8 **it was to be their treat:** seria a convite deles • 9 **along this line**: na mesma linha • 10 **tablecloths**: toalhas de mesa

painted chairs—with sweating glass water pitchers[1] and high, whirring fans[2], he picked up a table napkin[3] the size of a diaper[4] and spoke to me in a loud whisper, "Can you tell me what to do with this thing? Can I put it on my head to keep the draft off[5]?"

Of course he had eaten in hotel dining rooms before. He knew about table napkins and pie forks[6]. And my mother knew—she wasn't even a country woman, to begin with. Nevertheless[7] this was a huge event[8]. Not exactly a pleasure—as Beryl must have meant it to be[9]—but a huge, unsettling[10] event. Eating a meal in public, only a few miles from home, eating in a big room full of people you didn't know, the food served by a stranger, a snippy-looking[11] girl who was probably a college student working at a summer job.

"I'd like the rooster[12]," my father said. "How long has he been in the pot[13]?" It was only good manners, as he knew it, to joke with people who waited on him[14].

"Beg your pardon[15]?" the girl said.

"Roast chicken[16]," said Beryl. "Is that okay for everybody?"

1 **sweating glass water pitchers:** jarras de água com gotas de condensação • 2 **whirring fans:** ventiladores zumbindo • 3 **napkin:** guardanapo • 4 **diaper:** fralda • 5 **to keep the draft off:** para me proteger da corrente de ar • 6 **pie forks:** talheres de sobremesa • 7 **nevertheless**: no entanto • 8 **a huge event:** um acontecimento muito importante • 9 **as Beryl must have meant it to be:** como Beryl pretendia que fosse • 10 **unsettling:** perturbador • 11 **snippy-looking:** de aspecto insolente • 12 **I'd like the rooster:** o galo para mim • 13 **pot:** panela • 14 **it was only good manners, as he knew it, to joke with people who waited on him:** era de bom tom, na visão dele, "brincar" com quem lhe servia • 15 **beg your pardon?:** perdão? • 16 **roast chicken:** frango assado

Mr. Florence was looking gloomy[1]. Perhaps he didn't care for jokes[2] when it was his money that was being spent. Perhaps he had counted on something better than ice water to fill up the glasses.

The waitress put down a dish of celery[3] and olives, and my mother said, "Just a minute while I give thanks." She bowed[4] her head and said quietly but audibly, "Lord, bless[5] this food to our use, and us to Thy[6] service, for Christ's sake[7]. Amen." Refreshed, she sat up straight[8] and passed the dish to me, saying, "Mind[9] the olives. There's stones in them."

Beryl was smiling around at the room.

The waitress came back with a basket of rolls[10].

"Parker House[11]!" Beryl leaned over[12] and breathed in their smell. "Eat them while they're hot enough to melt the butter!"

Mr. Florence twitched, and peered into the butter dish. "Is that what this is—butter? I thought it was Shirley Temple's curls[13]."

His face was hardly[14] less gloomy than before, but it was a joke, and his making it[15] seemed to convey[16] to us something of the very thing[17] that had just been publicly asked for—a blessing[18].

1 **gloomy:** desanimado • 2 **he didn't care for jokes:** não achava graça nas brincadeiras • 3 **put down a dish of celery:** serviu um prato de aipo • 4 **she bowed**: inclinou • 5 **bless:** abençoe • 6 **Thy:** Vosso (forma antiga) • 7 **for Christ's sake:** em nome de Cristo • 8 **she sat up straight:** endireitou-se • 9 **mind:** cuidado com • 10 **a basket of rolls:** uma cesta de pãezinhos • 11 **Parker House:** tipo de pãozinho • 12 **leaned over:** inclinou-se • 13 **curls:** cachos • 14 **hardly:** mal; pouco • 15 **his making it:** o fato de tê-la feito • 16 **to convey:** transmitir • 17 **something of the very thing:** algo daquilo que precisamente • 18 **a blessing:** uma bênção

"When he says something funny," said Beryl—who often referred to Mr. Florence as "he" even when he was right there[1]—"you notice how he always keeps a straight face[2]? That reminds me of Mama. I mean of our mama, Marietta's and mine. Daddy, when he made a joke you could see it coming a mile away[3]—he couldn't keep it off his face[4]—but Mama was another story. She could look so sour[5]. But she could joke on her deathbed[6]. In fact, she did that very thing. Marietta, remember when she was in bed in the front room the spring before she died?"

"I remember she was in bed in that room," my mother said. "Yes."

"Well, Daddy came in and she was lying there in her clean nightgown, with the covers off[7], because the German lady from next door[8] had just been helping her take a wash, and she was still there tidying up the bed[9]. So Daddy wanted to be cheerful[10], and he said, 'Spring must be coming. I saw a crow[11] today.' This must have been in March. And Mama said quick as a shot[12], 'Well, you better cover me up then[13], before it looks in that window and gets any ideas[14]!' The German lady—Daddy said she just about dropped the basin[15].

1 **right there:** ali mesmo • 2 **he always keeps a straight face:** está sempre sério • 3 **you could see it coming a mile away:** podia vê-la chegando de longe • 4 **he couldn't keep it off his face:** não podia dissimular • 5 **she could look so sour:** podia parecer tão azeda • 6 **deathbed:** leito de morte • 7 **with the covers off:** sem as cobertas • 8 **lady from next door:** vizinha • 9 **tidying up the bed:** arrumando a cama • 10 **cheerful:** alegre • 11 **crow:** corvo • 12 **quick as a shot:** rápida como um raio • 13 **you better cover me up then:** então é melhor você me cobrir • 14 **gets any ideas:** tenha alguma ideia • 15 **she just about dropped the basin:** quase deixou cair a bacia

Because it was true, Mama was skin and bones[1]; she was dying. But she could joke."

Mr. Florence said, "Might as well when there's no use to cry[2]."

"But she could carry a joke too far[3], Mama could. One time, one time, she wanted to give Daddy a scare[4]. He was supposed to be interested in some girl that kept coming around to the works[5]. Well, he was a big good-looking man. So Mama said, 'Well, I'll just do away with myself[6], and you can get on with her[7] and see how you like it[8] when I come back and haunt[9] you.' He told her not to be so stupid, and he went off downtown. And Mama went out to the barn and climbed on a chair and put a rope around her neck. Didn't she, Marietta? Marietta went looking for her and she found her like that!"

My mother bent[10] her head and put her hands in her lap[11], almost as if she was getting ready to say another grace[12].

"Daddy told me all about it[13], but I can remember anyway. I remember Marietta tearing off[14] down the hill in her nightie[15], and I guess the German lady saw her go, and she

1 **was skin and bones:** estava pele e osso • 2 **might as well when there's no use to cry:** é melhor, quando não adianta chorar • 3 **she could carry a joke too far:** podia levar uma piada longe demais • 4 **a scare:** um susto • 5 **kept coming around to the works:** aparecia com frequência na fábrica • 6 **I'll just do away with myself:** me suicidarei • 7 **you can get on with her:** pode ficar com ela • 8 **and see how you like it:** e ver se você gosta • 9 **haunt:** assombrar • 10 **bent:** inclinou • 11 **lap:** regaço, colo • 12 **as if she was getting ready to say another grace:** como se se preparasse para uma nova bênção • 13 **told me all about it:** me contou tudo • 14 **tearing off:** saindo em disparada • 15 **nightie:** camisola

came out and was looking for Mama, and somehow we all ended up[1] in the barn—me too, and some kids I was playing with—and there was Mama up on a chair preparing to give Daddy the fright of his life[2]. She'd sent Marietta after him[3]. And the German lady starts wailing[4], 'Oh, missus, come down missus, think of your little *kindren*'—'*kindren*' is the German for 'children'—'think of your *kindren,*' and so on[5]. Until it was me standing there—I was just a little squirt[6], but I was the one noticed that rope[7]. My eyes followed that rope up and up and I saw it was just hanging over the beam[8], just flung there[9]—it wasn't tied[10] at all! Marietta hadn't noticed that, the German lady hadn't noticed it. But I just spoke up and said[11], 'Mama, how are you going to manage[12] to hang yourself without that rope tied around the beam?' "

Mr. Florence said, "That'd be a tough one[13]."

"I spoiled her game[14]. The German lady made coffee and we went over there and had a few treats[15], and, Marietta, you couldn't find Daddy after all[16], could you? You could hear Marietta howling[17], coming up the hill, a block away[18]."

"Natural for her to be upset," my father said.

1 **ended up:** fomos parar • 2 **the fright of his life:** o susto da vida dele • 3 **she'd sent Marietta after him:** mandou Marietta ir buscá-lo • 4 **starts wailing:** começa a gritar • 5 **and so on:** etc. • 6 **I was just a little squirt**: era só um "palitinho" • 7 **I was the one that noticed that rope:** mas fui eu quem reparou na corda • 8 **hanging over the beam:** pendurada na viga • 9 **just flung there:** só jogada por cima • 10 **tied:** amarrada • 11 **I just spoke up and said:** levantei a voz e disse • 12 **to manage:** conseguir • 13 **that'd be a tough one:** isso, sim, seria difícil • 14 **I spoiled her game:** acabei com a sua festa • 15 **treats:** guloseimas • 16 **after all:** no fim das contas • 17 **howling:** berrando • 18 **a block away:** a um quarteirão de distância

"Sure it was. Mama went too far[1]."

"She meant it," my mother said. "She meant it more than you give her credit for[2]."

"She meant to get a rise out of Daddy[3]. That was their whole life together. He always said she was a hard woman to live with, but she had a lot of character. I believe he missed that[4], with Gladys."

"I wouldn't know," my mother said, in that particularly steady voice[5] with which she always spoke of her father. "What he did say or didn't say."

"People are dead now," said my father. "It isn't up to us to judge[6]."

"I know," said Beryl. "I know Marietta's always had a different view[7]."

My mother looked at Mr. Florence and smiled quite easily and radiantly. "I'm sure you don't know what to make of all these family matters[8]."

The one time that I visited Beryl, when Beryl was an old woman, all knobby and twisted up[9] with arthritis, Beryl said, "Marietta got all Daddy's looks[10]. And she never did a thing with herself[11]. Remember her wearing that old navy-blue

1 **went too far:** foi longe demais • 2 **she meant it more than you give her credit for:** ela falava mais sério do que parecia • 3 **to get a rise out of Daddy:** fazer o papai perder as estribeiras • 4 **he missed that:** ele sentia falta disso • 5 **steady voice:** voz serena • 6 **it isn't up to us to judge:** não cabe a nós julgar • 7 **view:** ponto de vista • 8 **you don't know what to make of all these family matters:** não sabe o que pensar de todos esses assuntos familiares • 9 **knobby and twisted up:** ossuda e torta • 10 **got all Daddy's looks:** herdou a beleza do papai • 11 **she never did a thing with herself:** ela nunca se cuidou

crêpe dress[1] when we went to the hotel that time? Of course, I know it was probably all she had, but did it have to be all she had? You know, I was scared of her somehow. I couldn't stay in a room alone with her. But she had outstanding[2] looks." Trying to remember an occasion when I had noticed my mother's looks, I thought of the time in the hotel, my mother's pale-olive[3] skin against the heavy white, coiled hair[4], her open, handsome[5] face smiling at Mr. Florence—as if[6] he was the one to be forgiven[7].

I didn't have a problem right away[8] with Beryl's story. For one thing, I was hungry and greedy[9], and a lot of my attention went to the roast chicken and gravy[10] and mashed potatoes[11] laid on the plate with an ice-cream scoop[12] and the bright diced vegetables out of a can[13], which I thought much superior to those fresh from the garden. For dessert, I had a butterscotch sundae[14], an agonizing choice over chocolate. The others had plain vanilla ice cream.

Why shouldn't Beryl's version of the same event be different from my mother's? Beryl was strange in every way—everything about her was slanted[15], seen from a new

1 **navy-blue crêpe dress:** vestido azul-marinho de crepe • 2 **outstanding:** extraordinária • 3 **pale-olive:** cor de azeitona clara • 4 **coiled hair:** cabelo preso • 5 **handsome:** bonito • 6 **as if:** como se • 7 **forgiven:** perdoado • 8 **right away:** no momento • 9 **greedy:** gulosa • 10 **gravy:** molho de carne • 11 **mashed potatoes:** purê de batatas • 12 **laid on the plate with an ice cream scoop:** servido no prato com uma colher de sorvete • 13 **bright diced vegetables out of a can:** verduras brilhantes cortadas em cubo saídas de uma lata • 14 **butterscotch sundae:** *sundae* de caramelo • 15 **slanted:** distorcido

angle. It was my mother's version that held[1], for a time. It absorbed Beryl's story, closed over it. But Beryl's story didn't vanish[2]; it stayed sealed off[3] for years, but it wasn't gone. It was like the knowledge of that hotel and dining room. I knew about it now, though I didn't think of it as a place to go back to. And indeed, without Beryl's or Mr. Florence's money, I couldn't. But I knew it was there.

The next time I was in the Wildwood Inn, in fact, was after I was married. The Lions Club[4] had a banquet and dance there. The man I had married, Dan Casey, was a Lion. You could get a drink there by that time. Dan Casey wouldn't have gone anywhere you couldn't. Then the place was remodelled into the Hideaway, and now they have strippers every night but Sunday. On Thursday nights, they have a male stripper. I go there with people from the real-estate office to celebrate birthdays or other big events.

The farm was sold for five thousand dollars in 1965. A man from Toronto bought it, for a hobby farm or just an investment[5]. After a couple of years, he rented it[6] to a commune. They stayed there, different people drifting on and off[7], for a dozen years or so. They raised goats[8] and sold the milk to the health-food store[9] that had opened up in town. They painted a rainbow[10] across the side of the barn that faced the

1 **held:** prevaleceu • 2 **didn't vanish:** não desapareceu • 3 **sealed off:** selada • 4 **The Lions Club:** sociedade beneficente norte-americana • 5 **investment:** investimento • 6 **he rented it:** alugou-a • 7 **drifting on and off:** entravam e saíam • 8 **they raised goats:** criavam cabras • 9 **health-food store:** loja de comida natural • 10 **rainbow:** arco-íris

road. They hung tie-dyed sheets[1] over the windows, and let the long grass and flowering weeds reclaim the yard[2]. My parents had finally got electricity in, but these people didn't use it. They preferred oil lamps and the wood stove, and taking their dirty clothes to town. People said they wouldn't know how to handle[3] lamps or wood fires, and they would burn the place down[4]. But they didn't. In fact, they didn't manage badly[5]. They kept the house and barn in some sort of repair[6] and they worked a big garden. They even dusted their potatoes against blight[7]—though I heard that there was some sort of row[8] about this and some of the stricter members left. The place actually looked a lot better than many of the farms round about[9] that were still in the hands of the original families. The McAllister son had started a wrecking business[10] on their place. My own brothers were long gone[11].

I knew I was not being reasonable, but I had the feeling that I'd rather see the farm suffer outright neglect[12]—I'd sooner see it in the hands of hoodlums and scroungers[13]—than see that rainbow on the barn, and some letters that looked

1 **tie-dyed sheets**: lençóis tingidos com batique (em estilo *hippie*) • 2 **let the long grass and flowering weeds reclaim the yard:** deixaram a grama alta e as flores silvestres reconquistarem o jardim • 3 **how to handle:** como manusear • 4 **they would burn the place down:** incendiariam a casa • 5 **they didn't manage badly:** não se deram mal • 6 **in some sort of repair:** mais ou menos em bom estado • 7 **they even dusted their potatoes against blight:** inclusive pulverizaram as batatas contra pragas • 8 **row:** disputa; briga • 9 **round about:** ao redor; na região • 10 **a wrecking business:** um negócio de demolição • 11 **were long gone:** tinham ido embora fazia muito tempo • 12 **I'd rather see the farm suffer outright neglect:** preferiria ver a fazenda sofrer de total abandono • 13 **I'd sooner see it in the hands of hoodlums and scroungers:** preferiria vê-la nas mãos de vagabundos e ladrões

Egyptian painted on the wall of the house. They seemed a mockery[1]. I even disliked the sight of those people when they came to town—the men with their hair in ponytails[2], and with holes in their overalls[3] that I believed were cut on purpose[4], and the women with long hair and no makeup and their meek[5], superior expressions. What do you know about life, I felt like asking them. What makes you think you can come here and mock[6] my father and mother and their life and their poverty? But when I thought of the rainbow and those letters, I knew they weren't trying to mock or imitate my parents' life. They had displaced[7] that life, hardly knowing it existed. They had set up[8] in its place these beliefs and customs of their own, which I hoped would fail them[9].

That happened, more or less. The commune disintegrated. The goats disappeared. Some of the women moved to town, cut their hair, put on makeup, and got jobs as waitresses or cashiers[10] to support their children[11]. The Toronto man put the place up for sale[12], and after about a year it was sold for more than ten times what he had paid for it. A young couple from Ottawa bought it. They have painted the outside a pale gray with oyster trim[13], and have put in skylights[14] and a handsome front door with carriage lamps[15] on either side.

1 **mockery:** zombaria • 2 **ponytails:** rabos de cavalo • 3 **overalls:** macacões • 4 **on purpose:** de propósito • 5 **meek:** meiga • 6 **mock:** ridicularizar • 7 **they had displaced:** haviam substituído • 8 **they had set up:** haviam estabelecido • 9 **which I hoped would fail them:** que eu esperava que falhassem • 10 **cashiers:** encarregadas do caixa • 11 **to support their children:** para sustentar os filhos • 12 **put the place up for sale:** colocou o lugar à venda • 13 **oyster trim:** faixa cor de pérola • 14 **skylights:** claraboias • 15 **carriage lamps:** lanternas de carruagem

Inside, they've changed it around so much that I've been told I'd never recognize it.

I did get in once, before this happened, during the year that the house was empty and for sale. The company I work for was handling it[1], and I had a key, though the house was being shown by another agent. I let myself in[2] on a Sunday afternoon. I had a man with me, not a client but a friend—Bob Marks, whom I was seeing a lot at the time.

"This is that hippie place," Bob Marks said when I stopped the car. "I've been by here before."

He was a lawyer, a Catholic, separated from his wife. He thought he wanted to settle down and start up a practice[3] here in town. But there already was one Catholic lawyer. Business was slow. A couple of times a week, Bob Marks would be fairly drunk[4] before supper.

"It's more than that," I said. "It's where I was born. Where I grew up." We walked through the weeds, and I unlocked[5] the door.

He said that he had thought, from the way I talked, that it would be farther out[6].

"It seemed farther then."

All the rooms were bare[7], and the floors swept clean[8]. The woodwork was freshly painted—I was surprised to see no smudges[9] on the glass. Some new panes[10], some old wavy

1 **handling it:** cuidava da venda • 2 **I let myself in:** entrei • 3 **to settle down and start up a practice:** estabelecer-se e começar a exercer sua profissão • 4 **fairly drunk:** bastante bêbado • 5 **I unlocked:** destranquei a porta • 6 **farther out:** bem mais longe • 7 **bare:** vazios • 8 **swept clean:** varridos • 9 **smudges:** manchas • 10 **panes:** vidraças

ones. Some of the walls had been stripped of their paper and painted. A wall in the kitchen was painted a deep blue, with an enormous dove[1] on it. On a wall in the front room, giant sunflowers[2] appeared, and a butterfly[3] of almost the same size.

Bob Marks whistled[4]. "Somebody was an artist."

"If that's what you want to call it," I said, and turned back to the kitchen. The same wood stove was there. "My mother once burned up three thousand dollars," I said. "She burned three thousand dollars in that stove."

He whistled again, differently. "What do you mean? She threw[5] in a check?"

"No, no. It was in bills[6]. She did it deliberately. She went into town to the bank and she had them give it all to her, in a shoebox. She brought it home and put it in the stove. She put it in just a few bills at a time, so it wouldn't make too big a blaze[7]. My father stood and watched her."

"What are you talking about?" said Bob Marks. "I thought you were so poor."

"We were. We were very poor."

"So how come she had three thousand dollars? That would be like thirty thousand today. Easily. More than thirty thousand today."

"It was her legacy[8]," I said. "It was what she got from her father. Her father died in Seattle and left her three thousand dollars, and she burned it up because she hated him.

1 **dove:** pomba • 2 **sunflowers:** girassóis • 3 **butterfly:** borboleta • 4 **whistled:** assobiou • 5 **she threw:** jogou • 6 **bills:** notas • 7 **blaze:** labareda • 8 **legacy:** herança

She didn't want his money. She hated him."

"That's a lot of hate," Bob Marks said.

"That isn't the point. Her hating him, or whether he was bad enough for her to have a right to hate him. Not likely he was[1]. That isn't the point."

"Money," he said. "Money's always the point."

"No. My father letting her do it is the point. To me it is. My father stood and watched and he never protested. If anybody had tried to stop her, he would have protected her. I consider that love."

"Some people would consider it lunacy[2]."

I remember that that had been Beryl's opinion, exactly.

I went into the front room and stared at[3] the butterfly, with its pink-and-orange wings[4]. Then I went into the front bedroom and found two human figures painted on the wall. A man and a woman holding hands and facing straight ahead[5]. They were naked[6], and larger than life size[7].

"It reminds me of that John Lennon and Yoko Ono picture," I said to Bob Marks, who had come in behind me. "That record cover, wasn't it?[8]" I didn't want him to think that anything he had said in the kitchen had upset me.

Bob Marks said, "Different color hair."

That was true. Both figures had yellow hair painted in a solid mass, the way they do it in the comic strips[9]. Horsetails[10]

1 **not likely he was:** provavelmente não era • 2 **lunacy:** loucura • 3 **stared at:** olhei fixamente para • 4 **wings:** asas • 5 **facing straight ahead:** olhando de frente • 6 **naked:** nus • 7 **larger than life size:** maiores que o tamanho natural • 8 **that record cover, wasn't it?:** a capa daquele disco, não é? • 9 **comic strips:** histórias em quadrinhos • 10 **horsetails:** rabos de cavalo

of yellow hair curling over their shoulders and little pigs' tails of yellow hair decorating their not so private parts[1]. Their skin was a flat[2] beige pink and their eyes a staring blue[3], the same blue that was on the kitchen wall.

I noticed that they hadn't quite finished peeling the wall-paper away before making this painting. In the corner, there was some paper left that matched[4] the paper on the other walls—a modernistic design of intersecting pink and gray and mauve bubbles[5]. The man from Toronto must have put that on. The paper underneath hadn't been stripped off when this new paper went on. I could see an edge[6] of it, the corn-flowers[7] on a white ground.

"I guess this was where they carried on their sexual she-nanigans[8]," Bob Marks said, in a tone familiar to me. That thickened[9], sad, uneasy[10], but determined[11] tone. The not particularly friendly lust of middle-aged respectable men[12].

I didn't say anything. I worked away some of the bubble paper to see more of the cornflowers. Suddenly I hit a loose spot[13], and ripped away a big swatch[14] of it. But the corn-flower paper came too, and a little shower of dried plaster[15].

1 **their not so private parts:** suas partes não tão íntimas • 2 **flat:** opaco • 3 **a staring blue:** de um azul intenso • 4 **matched:** combinava • 5 **intersecting pink and gray and mauve bubbles:** bolhas de cor rosa, cinza e malva que se cruzam • 6 **an edge:** uma borda • 7 **cornflowers:** centáureas azuis • 8 **carried on their sexual shenanigans:** praticavam seus jogos sexuais • 9 **thickened:** denso • 10 **uneasy:** inquieto • 11 **determined:** determinado • 12 **the not particularly friendly lust of middle-aged respectable men:** a luxúria não muito agradável dos respeitáveis homens de meia-idade • 13 **loose spot:** ponto onde o papel estava solto • 14 **ripped away a big swatch:** arranquei um bom pedaço • 15 **plaster:** gesso

"Why is it?" I said. "Just tell me, why is it that no man can mention a place like this without getting around to[1] the subject of sex in about two seconds flat[2]? Just say the words "hippie" or "commune" and all you guys can think about is screwing[3]! As if there wasn't anything at all behind it but orgies and fancy combinations[4] and non-stop screwing! I get so sick of that[5]—it's all so stupid it just makes me sick!"

In the car, on the way home from the hotel, we sat as before —the men in the front seat, the women in the back. I was in the middle, Beryl and my mother on either side of me. Their heated bodies pressed against me, through cloth[6]; their smells crowded out[7] the smells of the cedar bush we passed through, and the pockets of bog[8], where Beryl exclaimed at the water lilies[9]. Beryl smelled of[10] all those things in pots and bottles. My mother smelled of flour[11] and hard soap and the warm crêpe of her good dress and the kerosene she had used to take the spots off[12].

"A lovely meal[13]," my mother said. "Thank you, Beryl. Thank you, Mr. Florence."

"I don't know who is going to be fit to do the milking[14]," my father said. "Now that we've all ate in such style."

1 **getting around to:** chegar ao assunto • 2 **two seconds flat:** exatos dois segundos • 3 **screwing:** transar • 4 **fancy combinations:** posições extravagantes • 5 **I get so sick of that:** me dá tanto nojo • 6 **cloth:** tecido • 7 **crowded out:** encobriam • 8 **pockets of bog:** zonas pantanosas • 9 **water lilies:** vitórias-régias • 10 **smelled of:** cheirava a • 11 **flour:** farinha • 12 **to take the spots off:** para tirar as manchas • 13 **a lovely meal:** uma refeição deliciosa • 14 **to be fit to do the milking:** estará em condições para a ordenha

"Speaking of money," said Beryl—though nobody actually had been—"do you mind my asking[1] what you did with yours? I put mine in real estate[2]. Real estate in California—you can't lose. I was thinking you could get an electric stove[3], so you wouldn't have to bother with[4] a fire in summer or fool with that coal-oil thing[5], either one."

All the other people in the car laughed, even Mr. Florence.

"That's a good idea, Beryl," said my father. "We could use it to set things on[6] till we get the electricity."

"Oh, Lord," said Beryl. "How stupid can I get?"

"And we don't actually[7] have the money, either," my mother said cheerfully[8], as if she was continuing the joke.

But Beryl spoke sharply[9]. "You wrote me you got it. You got the same as me."

My father half turned in his seat. "What money are you talking about?" he said. "What's this money?"

"From Daddy's will[10]," Beryl said. "That you got last year. Look, maybe I shouldn't have asked. If you had to pay something off[11], that's still a good use, isn't it? It doesn't matter. We're all family here. Practically."

"We didn't have to use it to pay anything off," my mother said. "I burned it."

1 **do you mind my asking:** você se importa se eu perguntar • 2 **I put mine in real estate:** investi o meu em imóveis • 3 **an electric stove:** um fogão elétrico • 4 **so you wouldn't have to bother with:** para que você não precise se preocupar com • 5 **fool with that coal-oil thing:** mexer com esse negócio de carvão • 6 **to set things on:** para colocar coisas em cima • 7 **actually:** na verdade • 8 **cheerfully:** alegremente • 9 **sharply:** com dureza • 10 **will:** testamento • 11 **to pay something off:** saldar uma dívida

Then she told how she went into town in the truck, one day almost a year ago, and got them to give her the money in a box she had brought along for the purpose[1]. She took it home, and put it in the stove and burned it.

My father turned around and faced the road ahead.

I could feel Beryl twisting[2] beside me while my mother talked. She was twisting, and moaning[3] a little, as if she had a pain[4] she couldn't suppress[5]. At the end of the story, she let out a sound of astonishment[6] and suffering, an angry groan[7].

"So you burned up money!" she said. "You burned up money in the stove."

My mother was still cheerful. "You sound as if I'd burned up one of my children."

"You burned their chances[8]. You burned up everything the money could have got for them."

"The last thing my children need is money. None of us need his money."

"That's criminal," Beryl said harshly[9]. She pitched[10] her voice into the front seat: "Why did you let her?"

"He wasn't there," my mother said. "Nobody was there."

My father said, "It was her money, Beryl."

"Never mind[11]," Beryl said. "That's criminal."

"Criminal is for when you call in the police," Mr. Florence said. Like other things he had said that day, this created a little island of surprise and a peculiar gratitude.

1 **she had brought along for the purpose:** que havia trazido com esse propósito • 2 **twisting:** se retorcendo • 3 **moaning:** gemendo • 4 **pain:** dor • 5 **suppress:** conter • 6 **astonishment:** estupefação • 7 **groan:** grunhido • 8 **chances:** oportunidades • 9 **harshly:** severamente • 10 **she pitched:** projetou • 11 **never mind:** não importa

Gratitude not felt by all.

"Don't you pretend[1] this isn't the craziest thing you ever heard of," Beryl shouted into the front seat. "Don't you pretend you don't think so! Because it is, and you do. You think just the same as me!"

My father did not stand in the kitchen watching my mother feed[2] the money into the flames. It wouldn't appear so[3]. He did not know about it—it seems fairly clear, if I remember everything, that he did not know about it until that Sunday afternoon in Mr. Florence's Chrysler, when my mother told them all together. Why, then, can I see the scene so clearly, just as I described it to Bob Marks (and to others—he was not the first)? I see my father standing by the table in the middle of the room—the table with the drawer[4] in it for knives and forks, and the scrubbed oilcloth[5] on top—and there is the box of money on the table. My mother is carefully dropping the bills into the fire. She holds the stove lid[6] by the blackened lifter[7] in one hand. And my father, standing by, seems not just to be permitting her to do this but to be protecting her. A solemn scene, but not crazy. People doing something that seems to them natural and necessary. At least, one of them is doing what seems natural and necessary, and the other believes that the important thing is for that person to be free, to go ahead. They understand that other people might not think so. They do not care.

1 **don't you pretend:** não finja que • 2 **feed:** introduzir • 3 **it wouldn't appear so:** parecia que não • 4 **drawer:** gaveta • 5 **the scrubbed oilcloth:** encerado gasto • 6 **the stove lid:** tampa do forno • 7 **the blackened lifter:** o puxador enegrecido

How hard it is for me to believe that I made that up[1]. It seems so much the truth it is the truth; it's what I believe about them. I haven't stopped believing it. But I have stopped telling that story. I never told it to anyone again after telling it to Bob Marks. I don't think so. I didn't stop just because it wasn't, strictly speaking, true. I stopped because I saw that I had to give up[2] expecting people to see it the way I did. I had to give up expecting them to approve of[3] any part of what was done. How could I even say that I approved of it myself? If I had been the sort of person who approved of that, who could do it, I wouldn't have done all I have done—run away[4] from home to work in a restaurant in town when I was fifteen, gone to night school to learn typing and bookkeeping, got into the real-estate office, and finally become a licensed agent. I wouldn't be divorced. My father wouldn't have died in the county home[5]. My hair would be white, as it has been naturally for years, instead of a color called Copper Sunrise[6]. And not one of these things would I change, not really, if I could.

Bob Marks was a decent man—good-hearted, sometimes with imagination. After I had lashed out at him[7] like that, he said, "You don't need to be so tough on us." In a moment, he said, "Was this your room when you were a little girl?" He thought that was why the mention of the sexual shenanigans had upset me.

1 **I made that up:** eu tinha inventado isso • 2 **I had to give up:** tinha que desistir de • 3 **to approve of:** aprovar • 4 **run away:** escapado • 5 **county home:** casa de beneficência do condado • 6 **Copper Sunrise:** amanhecer acobreado • 7 **after I had lashed out at him:** depois de tê-lo atacado

And I thought it would be just as well to let him think that. I said yes, yes, it was my room when I was a little girl. It was just as well to make up[1] right away. Moments of kindness and reconciliation are worth having, even if the parting[2] has to come sooner or later. I wonder if those moments aren't more valued, and deliberately gone after[3], in the setups[4] some people like myself have now, than they were in those old marriages, where love and grudges[5] could be growing underground, so confused and stubborn[6], it must have seemed they had forever.

1 **to make up:** fazer as pazes • 2 **the parting:** a despedida • 3 **gone after:** procurados • 4 **setups:** arranjos; acertos • 5 **grudges:** rancores • 6 **stubborn:** teimosos

Margaret Atwood

Death by Landscape

"She is entirely alive."

BIOGRAFIA

Margaret Atwood

Quando criança, não ia para a cama sem antes ter lido uma das histórias dos irmãos Grimm. *João e Maria* deve ter sido a sua favorita, com o bosque assustador e as crianças desamparadas.

Margaret Eleanor Atwood (Ottawa, Canadá, 1939) entende muito de bosques e crianças desamparadas. Não foi à escola até os 11 anos. Passou a sua infância de um lado para o outro, junto dos seus pais, sempre em busca do bosque mais fechado. Seu pai foi entomólogo florestal, daí a razão de dar voltas pelos bosques do Canadá. E "Death by Landscape" é uma boa amostra do fascínio de Margaret pela natureza. Na realidade, toda a sua produção literária o é.

Como não foi à escola, aprendeu a ler em casa. Tudo que fazia era ler. Aos seis anos escreveu seu primeiro conto e aos dezesseis já sabia claramente que queria ser escritora. Em 1961, formou-se na Universidade de Toronto. No mesmo ano ganhou o E. J. Pratt de poesia por *Double Persephone* [Perséfone dupla], um livro de poemas editado pela autora. Seu primeiro romance, *A mulher comestível*, só viria oito anos depois, em 1969. Um ano antes tinha se casado com Jim Polk, de quem se divorciou em 1973. Pouco depois conheceu o romancista Graeme Gibson, com quem teve uma filha em 1976. A essa altura, já havia escrito três romances (o último, *Madame oráculo*, uma paródia de contos de fadas), mais duas antologias de poesia e um ensaio literário. Atwood começava a construir seu universo, essencialmente feminino e feminista, e no qual destaca a preocupação pelo violento embate entre natureza e tecnologia, pelas relações entre Estados Unidos e Canadá e especialmente pela identidade canadense e os direitos humanos (o romance *Lesão corporal*, publicado em 1981, tem especial relevância nesse sentido).

Mas o tema amor sempre esteve ali. A primeira vez que tratou dos triângulos amorosos foi em *A vida antes do homem* (1979). Em seguida lançou uma das primeiras obras feministas escritas no Canadá, *Second Word*, de 1982. No mesmo ano dirigiu a revisão do *Oxford Book of Canadian Poetry*, o que a colocou à frente dos poetas canadenses de sua geração. Cinco anos depois ganharia o primeiro Arthur C. Clarke de ficção científica por *O conto da aia*, que narra a história de Offred, uma mulher-objeto da Nova República de Gilead (na verdade os velhos Estados Unidos açoitados por um regime teocrático neopuritano). Por essa obra Atwood foi considerada escritora de ficção científica, apesar de ela sempre ter recusado o título. "Não tem marcianos nem naves espaciais nos meus romances, só falo de uma sociedade que poderia existir ou ter existido", disse ela em uma ocasião. Prefere considerar sua prosa uma ficção especulativa e continuar dirigindo um carro híbrido (tanto ela quanto seu companheiro são ecologistas convictos).

Atualmente, Atwood, duas vezes ganhadora do Governor General's Award e do Booker (ganhou-o no ano 2000, graças a *O assassino cego*), dá aulas de escrita criativa em diversas universidades canadenses. Como se não bastasse, é autora de mais de dez coleções de contos, entre as quais se destaca *Wilderness Tips* [Dicas da vida na natureza] (1991), em que está incluída a cativante história "Death by Landscape".

APRESENTAÇÃO DO CONTO

Death by Landscape

Lois não é exatamente uma colecionadora de arte. Apesar de seus amigos acreditarem que ela tem um dom para descobrir os melhores quadros, se prestassem mais atenção, descobririam que o gosto de Lois pelas paisagens é doentio. A única coisa que ela vê quando os observa é algo que deixou para trás na sua infância durante uma excursão, enquanto brincavam de índios e pintavam a cara e subiam em canoas. Onde? No acampamento de verão. Até completar 9 anos, quando uma parte dela se perdeu para sempre no bosque, Lois passou todos os verões no acampamento Manitou. No início foi um pouco difícil (o racionamento de barras de chocolate lhe parecia especialmente cruel), mas acabou se acostumando. Fez uma amiga, Lucy, americana, sempre sorridente, que nunca se importava com o que pensavam dela. Viam-se todos os verões e durante o resto do ano se correspondiam por cartas em que se prometiam ser sempre amigas. Mas então aconteceu algo e tudo mudou de vez.

"Death by Landscape" foi publicado pela primeira vez em agosto de 1990 na revista *Harper's* e incluído um ano depois na coletânea de contos *Wilderness Tips*. A história de duas amigas em um acampamento de verão com a gélida paisagem canadense como pano de fundo poderia ser um clássico na literatura de Atwood – centrada, por um lado, na identidade canadense em si e como extensão do medo da natureza (os bosques estão por toda parte e parecem realmente perigosos), e, por outro, no sentimento de comunidade. A autora passou a infância adentrando bosques de todo tipo, sempre com um livro na mochila, e, quando cresceu, se dedicou a escrever sobre isso.

Seja qual for o caso, e apesar de a história não ter nada de sobrenatural (as distopias de ficção científica são uma das especialidades de Atwood), em "Death by Landscape" se condensa o universo particular e combativo da autora canadense, empenhada em apresentar-nos a paisagem como uma personagem a mais, quase sempre ameaçadora. E ela o faz de maneira tão sugestiva que cativa. E quando percebemos, já é tarde demais e não conseguimos parar de ler. Que diabos terá acontecido com as meninas? Que ocorreu naquele dia que saíram de canoa? Por que Lois ainda compra quadros de paisagens? Quem se esconde do outro lado?

Construído como um apanhado de lembranças que se sucedem no tempo (e na mente da narradora, a Lois criança, convertida em mãe de dois adolescentes), o conto extremamente afetuoso parece a narração de um diário pessoal, desses que um dia encontramos por acaso em uma velha gaveta e relemos. E nos surpreendemos ao ver o pouco que mudamos na realidade e o muito que havia de nós mesmos naquela menina que um dia fez uma amiga dos Estados Unidos e acreditou que podia mudar o mundo, nem que fosse por um segundo. O que segue, o fim do sonho, é a virada inesperada, porém inevitável, que acaba convertendo a vida da protagonista em uma tentativa de reter, como se retém um tesouro, pedaços de si mesma que captem o momento (a paisagem) do sonho desaparecido.

LAURA FERNÁNDEZ

Death by Landscape

NOW THAT THE BOYS are grown up and Rob is dead, Lois has moved to a condominium apartment[1] in one of the newer waterfront developments[2]. She is relieved not to have to worry about the lawn[3], or about the ivy[4] pushing its muscular little suckers[5] into the brickwork[6], or the squirrels gnawing their way into the attic[7] and eating the insulation off the wiring[8], or about strange noises. This building has a security system, and the only plant life is in pots[9] in the solarium.

Lois is glad she's been able to find an apartment big enough for her pictures. They are more crowded together[10] than they were in the house, but this arrangement gives the walls a European look: blocks of pictures, above and beside one another, rather than one over the chesterfield[11], one over the fireplace, one in the front hall, in the old acceptable manner of sprinkling art around[12] so it does not get too intrusive. This way has more of an impact. You know it's not supposed to be furniture.

1 **a condominium apartment:** prédio de apartamentos • 2 **waterfront developments:** empreendimentos em frente ao lago • 3 **lawn:** gramado • 4 **ivy:** hera • 5 **suckers:** gavinhas • 6 **brickwork:** alvenaria • 7 **the squirrels gnawing their way into the attic:** os esquilos roendo e abrindo caminho pelo sótão • 8 **eating the insulation off the wiring:** comendo a capa isolante da fiação • 9 **pots:** vasos • 10 **crowded together:** amontoadas • 11 **chesterfield:** tipo de sofá • 12 **sprinkling art around:** espalhar arte por aí

None of the pictures is very large, which doesn't mean they aren't valuable. They are paintings, or sketches[1] and drawings, by artists who were not nearly as well known when Lois began to buy them as they are now. Their work later turned up[2] on stamps[3], or as silk-screen reproductions[4] hung in the principals' offices of high schools, or as jigsaw puzzles[5], or on beautifully printed calendars sent out by corporations as Christmas gifts, to their less important clients. These artists painted mostly in the twenties and thirties and forties; they painted landscapes[6]. Lois has two Tom Thomsons, three A. Y. Jacksons, a Lawren Harris. She has an Arthur Lismer, she has a J. E. H. MacDonald. She has a David Milne. They are pictures of convoluted tree trunks[7] on an island of pink wave-smoothed stone[8], with more islands behind; of a lake with rough, bright, sparsely wooded cliffs[9]; of a vivid river shore[10] with a tangle of bush[11] and two beached canoes[12], one red, one grey; of a yellow autumn woods with the ice-blue gleam of a pond[13] half-seen through the interlaced branches[14].

It was Lois who'd chosen them. Rob had no interest in art, although he could see the necessity of having something on the walls. He left all the decorating decisions to her, while

1 **sketches:** esboços • 2 **turned up:** apareceu • 3 **stamps:** selos • 4 **silk-screen reproductions:** serigrafias • 5 **jigsaw puzzles:** quebra-cabeças • 6 **landscapes:** paisagens • 7 **convoluted tree trunks:** intrincados troncos de árvores • 8 **pink wave-smoothed stone:** pedra rosa gasta pelas ondas • 9 **sparsely wooded cliffs:** penhascos com árvores esparsas • 10 **shore:** beira • 11 **a tangle of bush:** um emaranhado de arbustos • 12 **two beached canoes:** duas canoas encalhadas • 13 **the ice-blue gleam of a pond:** o reflexo azul-claro de uma lagoa • 14 **half-seen through the interlaced branches:** vislumbrado entre os galhos entrelaçados

providing the money[1], of course. Because of this collection of hers, Lois's friends—especially the men—have given her the reputation of having a good nose for[2] art investments.

But this is not why she bought the pictures, way back then[3]. She bought them because she wanted them. She wanted something that was in them, although she could not have said at the time what it was. It was not peace: she does not find them peaceful in the least[4]. Looking at them fills her with a wordless unease[5]. Despite the fact that there are no people in them or even animals, it's as if there is something, or someone, looking back out[6].

When she was thirteen, Lois went on a canoe trip. She'd only been on overnights[7] before. This was to be a long one, into the trackless wilderness[8], as Cappie put it. It was Lois's first canoe trip, and her last.

Cappie was the head of the summer camp to which Lois had been sent ever since she was nine. Camp Manitou, it was called; it was one of the better ones, for girls, though not the best. Girls of her age whose parents could afford it were routinely packed off[9] to such camps, which bore a generic resemblance[10] to one another. They favoured[11] Indian names and had hearty, energetic leaders, who were called Cappie

1 **while providing the money:** enquanto providenciou o dinheiro • 2 **a good nose for:** um bom faro para • 3 **way back then:** naquele tempo • 4 **in the least:** em absoluto • 5 **a wordless unease:** um mal-estar inexplicável • 6 **looking back out:** devolvendo o olhar • 7 **overnights:** passeios de um dia para o outro • 8 **trackless wilderness:** natureza intocada • 9 **packed off:** enviadas • 10 **bore a generic resemblance:** possuíam uma semelhança genérica • 11 **they favoured:** costumavam ter

or Skip or Scottie. At these camps you learned to swim well and sail[1], and paddle[2] a canoe, and perhaps ride a horse or play tennis. When you weren't doing these things you could do Arts and Crafts and turn out dingy, lumpish clay ashtrays[3] for your mother—mothers smoked more, then—or bracelets made of coloured braided string[4].

Cheerfulness[5] was required at all times, even at breakfast. Loud shouting and the banging of spoons[6] on the tables were allowed, and even encouraged, at ritual intervals. Chocolate bars were rationed, to control tooth decay[7] and pimples[8]. At night, after supper, in the dining hall or outside around a mosquito-infested campfire ring for special treats[9], there were singsongs[10]. Lois can still remember all the words to "My Darling Clementine," and to "My Bonnie Lies Over the Ocean," with acting-out gestures: a rippling[11] of the hands for "the ocean," two hands together under the cheek for "lies". She will never be able to forget them, which is a sad thought.

Lois thinks she can recognize women who went to these camps, and were good at it. They have a hardness to their handshakes, even now; a way of standing, legs planted firmly and farther apart than usual; a way of sizing you up[12], to see if you'd be any good in a canoe—the front, not the back.

1 **sail:** navegar • 2 **paddle:** remar • 3 **turn out dingy, lumpish clay ashtrays:** fazer cinzeiros de barro toscos e foscos • 4 **braided string:** cordão trançado • 5 **cheerfulness:** alegria • 6 **banging of spoons:** o bater de colheres • 7 **tooth decay:** cáries • 8 **pimples:** espinhas • 9 **campfire ring for special treats:** fogueira para ocasiões especiais • 10 **there were singsongs:** havia cantoria • 11 **rippling:** ondulações • 12 **sizing you up:** medir com os olhos

They themselves would be in the back. They would call it the stern[1].

She knows that such camps still exist, although Camp Manitou does not. They are one of the few things that haven't changed much. They now offer copper enamelling[2], and functionless pieces of stained glass[3] baked in electric ovens, though judging from the productions of her friends' grandchildren the artistic standards have not improved.

To Lois, encountering it[4] in the first year after the war, Camp Manitou seemed ancient. Its log-sided[5] buildings with the white cement in between the half-logs, its flagpole ringed with whitewashed stones[6], its weathered grey dock jutting out[7] into Lake Prospect, with its woven rope bumpers[8] and its rusty rings for tying up[9], its prim round flowerbed[10] of petunias near the office door, must surely have been there always. In truth it dated only from the first decade of the century; it had been founded by Cappie's parents, who'd thought of camping as bracing[11] to the character, like cold showers, and had been passed along to her as an inheritance, and an obligation.

Lois realized, later, that it must have been a struggle[12] for Cappie to keep Camp Manitou going, during the Depression

1 **the stern:** a popa • 2 **copper enameling:** cobre esmaltado • 3 **stained glass:** vidro colorido • 4 **encountering it:** deparando • 5 **logsided:** construções com paredes de tronco • 6 **flagpole ringed with whitewashed stones:** haste da bandeira rodeada de pedras caiadas • 7 **weathered grey dock jutting out:** embarcadouro cinza desgastado pelo tempo que avançava • 8 **woven rope bumpers:** para-choques de cordas entrelaçadas • 9 **rusty rings for tying up:** argolas de amarrar enferrujadas • 10 **prim round flower-bed:** canteiros arredondados • 11 **bracing:** revigorante • 12 **struggle:** luta

and then the war, when money did not flow[1] freely. If it had been a camp for the very rich, instead of the merely well off[2], there would have been fewer problems. But there must have been enough Old Girls, ones with daughters, to keep the thing in operation, though not entirely shipshape[3]: furniture was battered[4], painted trim was peeling[5], roofs leaked[6]. There were dim[7] photographs of these Old Girls dotted around[8] the dining hall, wearing ample woolen[9] bathing suits and showing their fat, dimpled[10] legs, or standing, arms twined[11], in odd tennis outfits with baggy skirts[12].

In the dining hall, over the stone fireplace that was never used, there was a huge molting stuffed moose head[13], which looked somehow carnivorous. It was a sort of mascot; its name was Monty Manitou. The older campers spread the story that it was haunted[14], and came to life in the dark, when the feeble and undependable lights[15] had been turned off or, due to yet another generator failure, had gone out. Lois was afraid of it at first, but not after she got used to it.

Cappie was the same: you had to get used to her. Possibly she was forty, or thirty-five, or fifty. She had fawn-coloured[16] hair that looked as if it was cut with a bowl. Her head jutted

1 **did not flow:** não circulava • 2 **well off:** bem de vida • 3 **shipshape:** limpo e ordenado • 4 **furniture was battered:** os móveis estavam surrados • 5 **painted trim was peeling:** as molduras pintadas estavam descascando • 6 **roofs leaked:** os tetos tinham goteiras • 7 **dim:** escuras, apagadas • 8 **dotted around:** espalhadas • 9 **woolen:** de lã • 10 **dimpled:** cheias de celulite • 11 **arms twined:** de braços cruzados • 12 **baggy skirts:** saias largas • 13 **huge molting stuffed moose head:** enorme cabeça de alce empalhada que soltava pelos • 14 **haunted:** assombrada • 15 **feeble and undependable lights:** luzes fracas e pouco confiáveis • 16 **fawn-coloured:** castanho-amarelado

forward, jigging[1] like a chicken's as she strode[2] around the camp, clutching notebooks[3] and checking things off in them. She was like their minister in church: both of them smiled a lot and were anxious because they wanted things to go well; they both had the same overwashed skins and stringy necks[4]. But all this disappeared when Cappie was leading a singsong, or otherwise[5] leading. Then she was happy, sure of herself, her plain face almost luminous. She wanted to cause joy. At these times she was loved, at others merely trusted.

There were many things Lois didn't like about Camp Manitou, at first. She hated the noisy chaos and spoon-banging of the dining hall, the rowdy[6] singsongs at which you were expected to yell[7] in order to show that you were enjoying yourself. Hers was not a household[8] that encouraged yelling. She hated the necessity of having to write dutiful[9] letters to her parents claiming she was having fun. She could not complain, because camp cost so much money.

She didn't much like having to undress in a roomful of other girls, even in the dim light, although nobody paid any attention, or sleeping in a cabin with seven other girls, some of whom snored[10] because they had adenoids[11] or colds, some of whom had nightmares, or wet their beds[12] and cried about it. Bottom bunks[13] made her feel closed in, and she was

1 **jigging:** sacudindo • 2 **she strode:** caminhava • 3 **clutching notebooks:** segurando firmemente os cadernos • 4 **stringy necks:** pescoços fibrosos • 5 **otherwise:** de outra maneira • 6 **rowdy:** escandalosas • 7 **to yell:** gritar • 8 **household:** lar, casa • 9 **dutiful:** obedientes • 10 **snored:** roncavam • 11 **adenoids:** adenoides • 12 **wet their beds:** molhavam a cama • 13 **bottom bunks:** cama de baixo do beliche

afraid of falling out of top ones; she was afraid of heights. She got homesick[1], and suspected her parents of having a better time when she wasn't there than when she was, although her mother wrote to her every week saying how much they missed her. All this was when she was nine. By the time she was thirteen she liked it. She was an old hand[2] by then.

Lucy was her best friend at camp. Lois had other friends in winter, when there was school and itchy woollen clothing[3] and darkness in the afternoons, but Lucy was her summer friend.

She turned up the second year, when Lois was ten, and a Bluejay. (Chickadees, Bluejays, Ravens, and Kingfishers[4]—these were the names Camp Manitou assigned to the different age groups, a sort of totemic[5] clan system. In those days, thinks Lois, it was birds for girls, animals for boys: wolves, and so forth[6]. Though some animals and birds were suitable[7] and some were not. Never vultures[8], for instance; never skunks[9], or rats.)

Lois helped Lucy to unpack her tin trunk[10] and place the folded[11] clothes on the wooden shelves, and to make up her bed. She put her in the top bunk[12] right above her, where she could keep an eye on her. Already she knew that Lucy

1 **she got homesick:** estava com saudades da família • 2 **an old hand:** uma veterana • 3 **itchy woolen clothing:** roupa de lã que pinicava • 4 **Chickadees, Bluejays, Ravens and Kingfishers:** chickadees, gralhas-azuis, corvos e martins-pescadores • 5 **totemic:** totêmico • 6 **wolves and so forth:** lobos e outros • 7 **suitable:** adequados • 8 **vultures:** abutres • 9 **skunks:** gambás • 10 **to unpack her tin trunk:** desfazer o baú de latão • 11 **folded:** dobradas • 12 **top bunk:** cama de cima do beliche

was an exception, to a good many rules[1]; already she felt proprietorial[2].

Lucy was from the United States, where the comic books came from, and the movies. She wasn't from New York or Hollywood or Buffalo, the only American cities Lois knew the names of, but from Chicago. Her house was on the lake shore and had gates[3] to it, and grounds[4]. They had a maid[5], all of the time. Lois's family only had a cleaning lady twice a week.

The only reason Lucy was being sent to *this* camp (she cast a look[6] of minor scorn[7] around the cabin[8], diminishing it and also offending Lois, while at the same time daunting[9] her) was that her mother had been a camper here. Her mother had been a Canadian once, but had married her father, who had a patch over one eye, like a pirate. She showed Lois the picture of him in her wallet. He got the patch in the war. "Shrapnel[10]," said Lucy. Lois, who was unsure about shrapnel, was so impressed she could only grunt[11]. Her own two-eyed, unwounded[12] father was tame[13] by comparison.

"My father plays golf," she ventured[14] at last.

"*Everyone* plays golf," said Lucy. "My *mother* plays golf."

Lois's mother did not. Lois took Lucy to see the outhouses[15] and the swimming dock and the dining hall with Monty

1 **a good many rules:** muitas regras • 2 **she felt proprietorial:** se sentia dona • 3 **gates:** portões • 4 **grounds:** terras • 5 **a maid:** uma criada • 6 **she cast a look:** lançou um olhar • 7 **scorn:** desdém • 8 **cabin:** cabana • 9 **daunting:** intimidando • 10 **shrapnel:** metralha • 11 **grunt:** grunhir; resmungar • 12 **unwounded:** ileso • 13 **tame:** insosso • 14 **she ventured:** arriscou • 15 **outhouses:** banheiros externos

Manitou's baleful head[1], knowing in advance they would not measure up[2].

This was a bad beginning; but Lucy was good-natured[3], and accepted Camp Manitou with the same casual shrug[4] with which she seemed to accept everything. She would make the best of it, without letting Lois forget that this was what she was doing.

However, there were things Lois knew that Lucy did not. Lucy scratched[5] the tops off all her mosquito bites and had to be taken to the infirmary to be daubed[6] with Ozonol[7]. She took her T-shirt off while sailing, and although the counselor spotted her after a while and made her put it back on, she burnt spectacularly, bright red, with the X of her bathing-suit straps[8] standing out in alarming white; she let Lois peel the sheets of whispery-thin burned skin[9] off her shoulders. When they sang "Alouette" around the campfire, she did not know any of the French words. The difference was that Lucy did not care about[10] the things she didn't know, whereas Lois did.

During the next winter, and subsequent winters, Lucy and Lois wrote to each other. They were both only children, at a time when this was thought to be a disadvantage, so in their letters they pretended[11] to be sisters, or even twins[12]. Lois had

1 **baleful head:** cabeça sinistra • 2 **they would not measure up:** não estariam à altura • 3 **good-natured:** bondosa • 4 **casual shrug:** sacudir de ombros despreocupado • 5 **scratched:** coçava • 6 **daubed:** untada • 7 **Ozonol:** marca de pomada antibiótica • 8 **straps:** alças • 9 **peel the sheets of whispery-thin burned skin:** arrancar as finíssimas camadas de pele queimada • 10 **did not care about:** não se importava • 11 **they pretended:** fingiam • 12 **twins:** gêmeas

to strain[1] a little over this, because Lucy was so blond, with translucent skin and large blue eyes like a doll's, and Lois was nothing out of the ordinary—just a tallish, thinnish, brownish person with freckles[2]. They signed their letters LL, with the L's entwined together[3] like the monograms on a towel. (Lois and Lucy, thinks Lois. How our names date[4] us. Lois Lane, Superman's girlfriend, enterprising female reporter; "I Love Lucy." Now we are obsolete, and it's little Jennifers, little Emilys, little Alexandras and Carolines and Tiffanys.)

They were more effusive in their letters than they ever were in person. They bordered[5] their pages with X's and O's[6], but when they met again in the summers it was always a shock. They had changed so much, or Lucy had. It was like watching someone grow up in jolts[7]. At first it would be hard to think up things to say.

But Lucy always had a surprise or two, something to show, some marvel to reveal. The first year she had a picture of herself in a tutu, her hair in a ballerina's knot[8] on the top of her head; she pirouetted around the swimming dock to show Lois how it was done, and almost fell off. The next year she had given that up[9] and was taking horseback riding[10]. (Camp Manitou did not have horses.) The next year her mother and father had been divorced, and she had a new stepfather[11], one with both eyes, and a new house, although the maid was the same. The next year, when they had gradu-

1 **to strain:** esforçar-se • 2 **freckles:** sardas • 3 **entwined together:** entrelaçados • 4 **date:** revelam nossa idade • 5 **they bordered:** enchiam as margens • 6 **X's and O's (hugs and kisses):** beijos e abraços • 7 **in jolts:** aos solavancos • 8 **knot:** coque • 9 **she had given that up:** tinha abandonado • 10 **horseback riding:** equitação • 11 **stepfather:** padrasto

ated from Bluejays and entered Ravens, she got her period[1], right in the first week of camp. The two of them snitched[2] some matches from their counselor, who smoked illegally, and made a small fire out behind the farthest outhouse[3], at dusk[4], using their flashlights[5]. They could set all kinds of fires by now; they had learned how in Campcraft. On this fire they burned one of Lucy's used sanitary napkins[6]. Lois is not sure why they did this, or whose idea it was. But she can remember the feeling of deep satisfaction it gave her as the white fluff singed[7] and the blood sizzled[8], as if some wordless ritual had been fulfilled[9].

They did not get caught[10], but then they rarely got caught at any of their camp transgressions. Lucy had such large eyes, and was such an accomplished[11] liar.

This year Lucy is different again: slower, more languorous[12]. She is no longer interested in sneaking around[13] after dark, purloining[14] cigarettes from the counselor, dealing[15] in black-market candy bars[16]. She is pensive[17], and hard to wake in the mornings. She doesn't like her stepfather, but she doesn't want to live with her real father either, who has a new wife. She thinks her mother may be having a love affair[18] with a doctor; she doesn't know for sure, but she's

1 **period:** menstruação • 2 **snitched:** roubaram • 3 **the farthest outhouse:** a latrina mais distante • 4 **at dusk:** ao anoitecer • 5 **flashlights:** lanternas • 6 **sanitary napkins:** absorventes • 7 **the white fluff singed:** o felpo branco se chamuscava • 8 **the blood sizzled:** o sangue chiava • 9 **fulfilled:** cumprido • 10 **they did not get caught:** não foram pegas • 11 **accomplished:** bem-sucedida • 12 **languorous:** lânguida • 13 **sneaking around:** passear furtivamente • 14 **purloining:** roubando • 15 **dealing:** traficando • 16 **candy bars:** barras de chocolate • 17 **pensive:** pensativa • 18 **love affair:** caso amoroso

seen them smooching[1] in his car, out on the driveway[2], when her stepfather wasn't there. It serves him right[3]. She hates her private school. She has a boyfriend, who is sixteen and works as a gardener's assistant. This is how she met him: in the garden. She describes to Lois what it is like when he kisses her—rubbery[4] at first, but then your knees go limp[5]. She has been forbidden to see him, and threatened[6] with boarding school[7]. She wants to run away[8] from home.

Lois has little to offer in return. Her own life is placid and satisfactory, but there is nothing much that can be said about happiness. "You're so lucky," Lucy tells her, a little smugly[9]. She might as well say *boring* because this is how it makes Lois feel.

Lucy is apathetic[10] about the canoe trip, so Lois has to disguise[11] her own excitement. The evening before they are to leave, she slouches[12] into the campfire ring as if coerced[13], and sits down with a sigh of endurance[14], just as Lucy does.

Every canoe trip that went out of camp was given a special send-off[15] by Cappie and the section leader and counselors[16], with the whole section in attendance. Cappie painted three streaks[17] of red across each of her cheeks with a lipstick. They

1 **smooching:** beijando • 2 **driveway:** entrada da garagem • 3 **it serves him right:** ele merece • 4 **rubbery:** borrachento • 5 **your knees go limp:** os joelhos cambaleiam • 6 **threatened:** ameaçada • 7 **boarding school:** internato • 8 **to run away:** fugir • 9 **smugly:** convencida • 10 **apathetic:** apática • 11 **to disguise:** disfarçar • 12 **she slouches:** caminha arrastando os pés • 13 **as if coerced:** como que obrigada • 14 **a sigh of endurance:** suspiro de resignação • 15 **send-off:** despedida • 16 **counselors:** monitores • 17 **streaks:** listras

looked like three-fingered claw marks[1]. She put a blue circle on her forehead with fountain-pen ink[2], and tied a twisted bandanna[3] around her head and stuck a row of frazzle-ended feathers[4] around it, and wrapped herself in a red-and-black Hudson's Bay blanket[5]. The counselors, also in blankets but with only two streaks of red, beat on tom-toms[6] made of round wooden cheese boxes with leather stretched over the top and nailed in place[7]. Cappie was Chief Cappeosota. They all had to say "How!" when she walked into the circle and stood there with one hand raised.

Looking back on this, Lois finds it disquieting[8]. She knows too much about Indians: this is why. She knows, for instance, that they should not even be called Indians, and that they have enough worries without other people taking their names and dressing up[9] as them. It has all been a form of stealing.

But she remembers, too, that she was once ignorant of this. Once she loved the campfire, the flickering[10] of light on the ring of faces, the sound of the fake[11] tom-toms, heavy and fast like a scared heartbeat[12]; she loved Cappie in a red blanket and feathers, solemn, as a chief should be, raising her hand and saying, "Greetings[13], my Ravens." It was not

1 **three-fingered claw marks:** marcas de garras de três dedos • 2 **fountain-pen ink:** tinta de caneta-tinteiro • 3 **tied a twisted bandanna:** amarrou uma bandana torcida • 4 **stuck a row of frazzle-ended feathers:** cravou uma fileira de penas de pontas desgastadas • 5 **Hudson's Bay blanket:** cobertor da marca Hudson's Bay • 6 **beat on tom-toms:** tocavam tantãs • 7 **with leather stretched over the top and nailed in place:** com o couro esticado por cima • 8 **disquieting:** inquietante • 9 **dressing up:** fantasiando-se • 10 **flickering:** piscar • 11 **fake:** falsos • 12 **heartbeat:** batida do coração • 13 **greetings:** saudações

funny, it was not making fun. She wanted to be an Indian. She wanted to be adventurous and pure, and aboriginal.

"You go on big water," says Cappie. This is her idea—all their ideas—of how Indians talk. "You go where no man has ever trod[1]. You go many moons." This is not true. They are only going for a week, not many moons. The canoe route is clearly marked, they have gone over it on a map, and there are prepared campsites with names which are used year after year. But when Cappie says this—and despite the way Lucy rolls up her eyes[2]—Lois can feel the water stretching out[3], with the shores twisting away[4] on either side, immense and a little frightening.

"You bring back much wampum[5]," says Cappie. "Do good in war, my braves, and capture many scalps[6]." This is another of her pretenses[7]: that they are boys, and bloodthirsty[8]. But such a game cannot be played by substituting the word "squaw"[9]. It would not work at all.

Each of them has to stand up and step forward[10] and have a red line drawn across her cheeks[11] by Cappie. She tells them they must follow in the paths of their ancestors (who most certainly, thinks Lois, looking out the window of her apartment and remembering the family stash[12] of daguerreotypes

1 **has ever trod:** nunca pisou • 2 **rolls up her eyes:** revirou os olhos • 3 **stretching out:** alargando-se • 4 **the shores twisting away:** as margens afastando-se de cada lado • 5 **wampum:** contas utilizadas tradicionalmente pelos nativos norte-americanos como moeda • 6 **scalps:** escalpos • 7 **pretenses:** simulações • 8 **bloodthirsty:** sedentos de sangue • 9 **squaw:** mulher indígena • 10 **step forward:** dar um passo para a frente • 11 **cheeks:** bochechas • 12 **stash:** coleção

and sepia-coloured portraits[1] on her mother's dressing table[2], the stiff-shirted[3], black-coated[4], grim-faced[5] men and the beflounced[6] women with their severe hair[7] and their corseted respectability, would never have considered heading off[8] onto an open lake, in a canoe, just for fun).

At the end of the ceremony they all stood and held hands around the circle, and sang taps[9]. This did not sound very Indian, thinks Lois. It sounded like a bugle call[10] at a military post, in a movie. But Cappie was never one to be much concerned with consistency[11], or with archaeology.

After breakfast the next morning they set out[12] from the main dock, in four canoes, three in each. The lipstick stripes have not come off completely, and still show faintly[13] pink, like healing burns[14]. They wear their white denim[15] sailing hats, because of the sun, and thin-striped[16] T-shirts, and pale baggy[17] shorts with the cuffs rolled up[18]. The middle one kneels[19], propping her rear end[20] against the rolled sleeping bags. The counselors going with them are Pat and Kip. Kip is no-nonsense[21]; Pat is easier to wheedle[22], or fool[23].

1 **portraits:** retratos • 2 **dressing table:** penteadeira • 3 **stiff-shirted:** com camisas engomadas • 4 **black-coated:** com casacos pretos • 5 **grim-faced:** com expressão severa • 6 **beflounced:** de babados • 7 **severe hair:** cabelo austero • 8 **heading off:** dirigir-se • 9 **taps:** melodias militares de despedida • 10 **bugle call:** toque de cornetas • 11 **consistency:** coerência • 12 **they set out:** saíram • 13 **faintly:** ligeiramente • 14 **healing burns:** queimaduras se curando • 15 **denim:** jeans • 16 **thin-striped:** de listras finas • 17 **baggy:** soltos, folgados • 18 **with the cuffs rolled up:** com a barra dobrada • 19 **kneels:** se ajoelha • 20 **propping her rear end:** apoiando o traseiro • 21 **Kip is no-nonsense:** Kip é linha-dura • 22 **wheedle:** enrolar • 23 **fool:** enganar

There are white puffy clouds[1] and a small breeze. Glints[2] come from the little waves. Lois is in the bow[3] of Kip's canoe. She still can't do a J-stroke[4] very well, and she will have to be in the bow or the middle for the whole trip. Lucy is behind her; her own J-stroke is even worse. She splashes[5] Lois with her paddle, quite a big splash.

"I'll get you back[6]," says Lois.

"There was a stable fly[7] on your shoulder," Lucy says.

Lois turns to look at her, to see if she's grinning[8]. They're in the habit of splashing each other. Back there, the camp has vanished[9] behind the first long point of rock and rough trees[10]. Lois feels as if an invisible rope has broken. They're floating free, on their own, cut loose. Beneath the canoe the lake goes down, deeper and colder than it was a minute before.

"No horsing around[11] in the canoe," says Kip. She's rolled her T-shirt sleeves up[12] to the shoulder; her arms are brown and sinewy[13], her jaw[14] determined, her stroke perfect. She looks as if she knows exactly what she is doing.

The four canoes keep close together. They sing, raucously[15] and with defiance; they sing "The Quartermaster's Store," and "Clementine," and "Alouette." It is more like bellowing[16] than singing.

1 **white puffy clouds:** nuvens brancas fofas • 2 **glints:** brilhos • 3 **bow:** proa • 4 **J-stroke:** remar um J • 5 **she splashes:** salpicou • 6 **I'll get you back:** vou me vingar • 7 **a stable fly:** mosca-varejeira • 8 **she's grinning:** está sorrindo • 9 **has vanished:** desapareceu • 10 **rough trees:** árvores imperfeitas • 11 **horsing around:** brincadeiras • 12 **she's rolled her T-shirt sleeves up:** ela arregaçou as mangas da camiseta • 13 **sinewy:** vigorosos • 14 **jaw:** mandíbula • 15 **raucously:** escandalosamente • 16 **bellowing:** gritar

After that the wind grows stronger, blowing slantwise[1] against the bows[2], and they have to put all their energy into shoving[3] themselves through the water.

Was there anything important, anything that would provide some sort of reason or clue[4] to what happened next? Lois can remember everything, every detail; but it does her no good[5].

They stopped at noon for a swim and lunch, and went on in the afternoon. At last they reached Little Birch, which was the first campsite for overnight. Lois and Lucy made the fire, while the others pitched the heavy canvas tents[6]. The fireplace was already there, flat stones piled into a U[7]. A burned tin can[8] and a beer bottle had been left in it. Their fire went out, and they had to restart it. "Hustle your bustle[9]," said Kip. "We're starving[10]."

The sun went down, and in the pink sunset[11] light they brushed their teeth and spat the toothpaste froth[12] into the lake. Kip and Pat put all the food that wasn't in cans into a packsack[13] and slung[14] it into a tree, in case of bears.

Lois and Lucy weren't sleeping in a tent. They'd begged to be allowed to sleep out[15]; that way they could talk without

1 **slantwise:** na diagonal • 2 **the bows:** as proas • 3 **shoving:** impulsionar • 4 **clue:** pista • 5 **it does her no good:** não lhe faz bem • 6 **pitched the heavy canvas tents:** montavam as pesadas barracas de lona • 7 **flat stones piled into a U:** pedras planas colocadas em U • 8 **tin can:** lata • 9 **hustle your bustle:** rápido • 10 **we're starving:** estamos famintos • 11 **sunset:** pôr do sol • 12 **spat the toothpaste froth:** cuspiram a espuma da pasta de dentes • 13 **packsack:** mochila • 14 **slung:** penduraram • 15 **they'd begged to be allowed to sleep out:** tinham pedido que as deixassem dormir fora

the others hearing. If it rained, they told Kip, they promised not to crawl[1] dripping[2] into the tent over everyone's legs: they would get under the canoes. So they were out on the point[3].

Lois tried to get comfortable inside her sleeping bag, which smelled of musty storage[4] and of earlier campers, a stale[5] salty sweetness. She curled herself up[6], with her sweater rolled up under her head for a pillow[7] and her flashlight inside her sleeping bag so it wouldn't roll away. The muscles of her sore[8] arms were making small pings[9], like rubber bands[10] breaking.

Beside her Lucy was rustling around[11]. Lois could see the glimmering[12] oval of her white face.

"I've got a rock poking[13] into my back," said Lucy.

"So do I," said Lois. "You want to go into the tent?" She herself didn't, but it was right to ask.

"No," said Lucy. She subsided[14] into her sleeping bag. After a moment she said, "It would be nice not to go back."

"To camp?" said Lois.

"To Chicago," said Lucy. "I hate it there."

"What about your boyfriend?" said Lois. Lucy didn't answer. She was either asleep or pretending to be[15].

1 **to crawl:** arrastar-se • 2 **dripping:** pingando • 3 **out on the point:** fora, no promontório • 4 **musty storage:** cheiro de guardado, mofado • 5 **stale:** ranço • 6 **she curled herself up:** enrolou-se • 7 **for a pillow:** fazendo de travasseiro • 8 **sore:** doloridos • 9 **pings:** espasmos • 10 **rubber bands:** elásticos • 11 **rustling around:** mexia-se • 12 **the glimmering oval:** forma oval e brilhante • 13 **poking:** cutucando • 14 **she subsided:** ficou quieta • 15 **either asleep or pretending to be:** dormindo ou fingindo estar dormindo

There was a moon, and a movement of the trees. In the sky there were stars, layers of stars that went down and down. Kip said that when the stars were bright like that instead of hazy[1] it meant bad weather later on. Out on the lake there were two loons[2], calling to each other in their insane, mournful[3] voices. At the time it did not sound like grief[4]. It was just background[5].

The lake in the morning was flat calm[6]. They skimmed along[7] over the glassy surface, leaving V-shaped trails[8] behind them; it felt like flying. As the sun rose higher it got hot, almost too hot. There were stable flies in the canoes, landing[9] on a bare arm or leg for a quick sting[10]. Lois hoped for wind.

They stopped for lunch at the next of the named campsites, Lookout[11] Point. It was called this because, although the site itself was down near the water on a flat shelf of rock[12], there was a sheer cliff[13] nearby and a trail that led up to the top. The top was the lookout, although what you were supposed to see from there was not clear. Kip said it was just a view.

Lois and Lucy decided to make the climb[14] anyway. They didn't want to hang around[15] waiting for lunch. It wasn't their turn to cook, though they hadn't avoided much by not doing it, because cooking lunch was no big deal[16], it was just

1 **hazy:** com neblina • 2 **loons:** um tipo de gaivota • 3 **mournful:** queixosas • 4 **grief:** pena • 5 **background:** ruído de fundo • 6 **flat calm:** completamente calmo • 7 **they skimmed along:** passavam deslizando • 8 **V-shaped trails:** rastros em forma de V • 9 **landing:** pousando • 10 **sting:** picada • 11 **lookout:** mirante • 12 **a flat shelf of rock:** um recife achatado de rochas • 13 **sheer cliff:** penhasco íngreme • 14 **the climb:** escalada • 15 **to hang around:** perder tempo • 16 **was no big deal:** não era grande coisa

unwrapping[1] the cheese and getting out the bread and peanut butter, but Pat and Kip always had to do their woodsy act[2] and boil up[3] a billy tin[4] for their own tea.

They told Kip where they were going. You had to tell Kip where you were going, even if it was only a little way into the woods to get dry twigs for kindling[5]. You could never go anywhere without a buddy[6].

"Sure," said Kip, who was crouching[7] over the fire, feeding driftwood[8] into it. "Fifteen minutes to lunch."

"Where are they off to?" said Pat. She was bringing their billy tin of water from the lake.

"Lookout," said Kip.

"Be careful," said Pat. She said it as an afterthought[9], because it was what she always said.

"They're old hands," Kip said.

Lois looks at her watch: it's ten to twelve. She is the watch-minder[10]; Lucy is careless of time[11]. They walk up the path, which is dry earth and rocks, big rounded pinky-gray boulders[12] or split-open[13] ones with jagged edges[14]. Spindly balsam and spruce trees[15] grow to either side, the lake is blue

1 **unwrapping:** desembalar • 2 **woodsy act:** seu show de acampamento • 3 **boil up:** ferver • 4 **billy tin:** panela de camping • 5 **to get dry twigs for kindling:** pegar gravetos secos para acender o fogo • 6 **buddy:** companheiro • 7 **crouching:** de cócoras • 8 **driftwood:** madeira à deriva • 9 **afterthought:** pensamento tardio • 10 **watch-minder:** responsável pelo relógio • 11 **is careless of time:** não se importava com o tempo • 12 **boulders:** rochas • 13 **split-open:** partidas • 14 **jagged edges:** bordas irregulares • 15 **spindly balsam and spruce trees:** abetos balsâmicos e pinheiros

fragments to the left. The sun is right overhead; there are no shadows anywhere. The heat comes up at them as well as down. The forest is dry and crackly[1].

It isn't far, but it's a steep[2] climb and they're sweating[3] when they reach the top. They wipe[4] their faces with their bare arms, sit gingerly[5] down on a scorching-hot rock[6], five feet from the edge[7] but too close for Lois. It's a lookout all right, a sheer drop[8] to the lake and a long view over the water, back the way they've come. It's amazing to Lois that they've travelled so far, over all that water, with nothing to propel them[9] but their own arms. It makes her feel strong. There are all kinds of things she is capable of doing.

"It would be quite a dive[10] off here[11]," says Lucy.

"You'd have to be nuts[12]," says Lois.

"Why?" says Lucy. "It's really deep. It goes straight down." She stands up and takes a step nearer the edge. Lois gets a stab in her midriff[13], the kind she gets when a car goes too fast over a bump[14]. "Don't," she says.

"Don't what?" says Lucy, glancing around at her mischievously[15]. She knows how Lois feels about heights[16]. But she turns back. "I really have to pee[17]," she says.

"You have toilet paper?" says Lois, who is never without it. She digs[18] in her shorts pocket.

1 **crackly:** barulhenta • 2 **steep:** íngreme • 3 **they're sweating:** estão transpirando • 4 **they wipe:** enxugam • 5 **gingerly:** com cuidado • 6 **a scorching-hot rock:** uma rocha escaldante • 7 **edge:** borda • 8 **sheer drop:** uma queda vertiginosa • 9 **to propel them:** propeli-las • 10 **a dive:** um mergulho • 11 **off here:** desde aqui • 12 **nuts:** louca • 13 **a stab in her midriff:** uma pontada no estômago • 14 **bump:** lombada • 15 **glancing around at her mischievously:** lançando um olhar travesso na sua direção • 16 **heights:** alturas • 17 **to pee:** fazer xixi • 18 **she digs:** ela procura

"Thanks," says Lucy.

They are both adept at[1] peeing in the woods: doing it fast so the mosquitoes don't get you, the underwear[2] pulled up between the knees, the squat[3] with the feet apart so you don't wet your legs, facing downhill. The exposed feeling of your bum[4], as if someone is looking at you from behind. The etiquette when you're with someone else is not to look. Lois stands up and starts to walk back down the path, to be out of sight[5].

"Wait for me?" says Lucy.

Lois climbed down, over and around the boulders, until she could not see Lucy; she waited. She could hear the voices of the others, talking and laughing, down near the shore. One voice was yelling, "Ants[6]! Ants!" Someone must have sat on an ant hill[7]. Off to the side, in the woods[8], a raven was croaking[9], a hoarse[10] single note.

She looked at her watch: it was noon[11]. This is when she heard the shout[12].

She has gone over and over[13] it in her mind since, so many times that the first, real shout has been obliterated[14], like a footprint trampled by other footprints[15]. But she is sure (she is almost positive, she is nearly certain) that it was not a shout

1 **adept at:** craques em • 2 **underwear:** roupa de baixo • 3 **squat:** flexão de pernas • 4 **bum:** traseiro • 5 **to be out of sight:** não estar à vista • 6 **ants:** formigas • 7 **ant hill:** formigueiro • 8 **in the woods:** no bosque • 9 **a raven was croaking:** um corvo grasnava • 10 **hoarse:** rouca • 11 **noon:** meio-dia • 12 **the shout:** o grito • 13 **she was gone over and over:** relembrou tantas e tantas vezes • 14 **obliterated:** apagado • 15 **like a footprint trampled by other footprints:** como uma pegada pisoteada por outras

of fear. Not a scream[1]. More like a cry[2] of surprise, cut off[3] too soon. Short, like a dog's bark[4].

"Lucy?" Lois said. Then she called "Lucy!" By now she was clambering back up[5], over the stones of the path[6]. Lucy was not up there. Or she was not in sight.

"Stop fooling around[7]," Lois said. "It's lunchtime." But Lucy did not rise[8] from behind a rock or step out, smiling, from behind a tree. The sunlight was all around; the rocks looked white. "This isn't funny!" Lois said, and it wasn't, panic was rising in her, the panic of a small child who does not know where the bigger ones are hidden[9]. She could hear her own heart. She looked quickly around; she lay down on the ground and looked over the edge of the cliff. It made her feel cold. There was nothing.

She went back down the path, stumbling[10]; she was breathing too quickly; she was too frightened to cry. She felt terrible—guilty and dismayed[11], as if she had done something very bad, by mistake. Something that could never be repaired. "Lucy's gone," she told Kip.

Kip looked up from her fire, annoyed[12]. The water in the billy can was boiling. "What do you mean, gone?" she said. "Where did she go?"

"I don't know," said Lois. "She's just gone."

No one had heard the shout, but then no one had heard

1 **scream:** grito • 2 **cry:** exclamação • 3 **cut off:** interrompido • 4 **a dog's bark:** latido de cachorro • 5 **she was clambering back up:** escalava novamente • 6 **path:** caminho • 7 **stop fooling around:** pare de brincadeira • 8 **did not rise:** não se levantou • 9 **are hidden:** estão escondidos • 10 **stumbling:** tropeçando • 11 **dismayed:** assustada • 12 **annoyed:** incomodada

Lois calling, either. They had been talking among themselves, by the water.

Kip and Pat went up to the lookout and searched and called, and blew their whistles[1]. Nothing answered.

Then they came back down, and Lois had to tell exactly what had happened. The other girls all sat in a circle and listened to her. Nobody said anything. They all looked frightened, especially Pat and Kip. They were the leaders. You did not just lose a camper like this, for no reason at all.

"Why did you leave her alone?" said Kip.

"I was just down the path," said Lois. "I told you. She had to go to the bathroom." She did not say *pee* in front of people older than herself.

Kip looked disgusted[2].

"Maybe she just walked off into the woods and got turned around[3]," said one of the girls.

"Maybe she's doing it on purpose[4]," said another.

Nobody believed either of these theories.

They took the canoes and searched around the base of the cliff, and peered[5] down into the water. But there had been no sound of falling rock; there had been no splash[6]. There was no clue, nothing at all. Lucy had simply vanished.

That was the end of the canoe trip. It took them the same two days to go back that it had taken coming in, even though they were short a paddler[7]. They did not sing.

1 **blew their whistles:** tocaram seus apitos • 2 **disgusted:** indignada • 3 **got turned around:** se desorientou • 4 **on purpose:** de propósito • 5 **peered:** vasculharam • 6 **splash:** barulho de algo caindo na água • 7 **they were short a paddler:** estivesse com um remador a menos

After that, the police went in a motorboat, with dogs; they were the Mounties[1] and the dogs were German shepherds[2], trained to follow trails in the woods. But it had rained since, and they could find nothing.

Lois is sitting in Cappie's office. Her face is bloated with crying[3], she's seen that in the mirror. By now she feels numbed[4]; she feels as if she has drowned[5]. She can't stay here. It has been too much of a shock. Tomorrow her parents are coming to take her away. Several of the other girls who were on the canoe trip are also being collected. The others will have to stay, because their parents are in Europe, or cannot be reached[6].

Cappie is grim[7]. They've tried to hush it up[8], but of course everyone in camp knows. Soon the papers[9] will know too. You can't keep it quiet, but what can be said? What can be said that makes any sense? "Girl vanishes in broad daylight[10], without a trace[11]." It can't be believed. Other things, worse things, will be suspected. Negligence, at the very least. But they have always taken such care. Bad luck will gather[12] around Camp Manitou like a fog[13]; parents will avoid it, in favour of other, luckier places. Lois can see Cappie thinking all this, even through her numbness[14]. It's what anyone would think.

1 **the Mounties:** a Polícia Montada • 2 **German shepherds:** pastores-alemães • 3 **bloated with crying:** inchada de chorar • 4 **numbed:** confusa • 5 **she has drowned:** tivesse se afogado • 6 **cannot be reached:** não podem ser localizados • 7 **grim:** muito séria • 8 **to hush it up:** abafar a situação • 9 **papers:** jornais • 10 **in broad daylight:** em plena luz do dia • 11 **without a trace:** sem deixar rastro • 12 **will gather:** se concentrará • 13 **fog:** neblina • 14 **numbness:** atordoamento

Lois sits on the hard wooden chair in Cappie's office, beside the old wooden desk, over which hangs the thumbtacked bulletin board[1] of normal camp routine, and gazes[2] at Cappie through her puffy eyelids[3]. Cappie is now smiling what is supposed to be a reassuring[4] smile. Her manner is too casual: she's after something. Lois has seen this look on Cappie's face when she's been sniffing out[5] contraband chocolate bars, hunting down[6] those rumored to have snuck out[7] of their cabins at night.

"Tell me again," says Cappie, "from the beginning."

Lois has told her story so many times by now, to Pat and Kip, to Cappie, to the police, that she knows it word for word. She knows it, but she no longer[8] believes it. It has become a story. "I told you," she said. "She wanted to go to the bathroom. I gave her my toilet paper. I went down the path, I waited for her. I heard this kind of shout . . ."

"Yes," says Cappie, smiling confidingly, "but before that. What did you say to one another?"

Lois thinks. Nobody has asked her this before. "She said you could dive off there. She said it went straight down."

"And what did you say?"

"I said you'd have to be nuts."

"Were you mad at[9] Lucy?" says Cappie, in an encouraging[10] voice.

1 **thumbtacked bulletin board:** mural de anúncios cheios de tachinhas • 2 **gazes:** olha • 3 **puffy eyelids:** pálpebras inchadas • 4 **reassuring:** tranquilizador • 5 **she's been sniffing out:** foi descoberta • 6 **hunting down:** perseguindo • 7 **snuck out:** saído às escondidas • 8 **no longer:** deixou de • 9 **mad at:** brava com • 10 **encouraging:** alentadora

"No," says Lois. "Why would I be mad at Lucy? I wasn't ever mad at Lucy." She feels like crying again. The times when she has in fact been mad at Lucy have been erased[1] already. Lucy was always perfect.

"Sometimes we're angry[2] when we don't know we're angry," says Cappie, as if to herself. "Sometimes we get really mad and we don't even know it. Sometimes we might do a thing without meaning to[3], or without knowing what will happen. We lose our tempers[4]."

Lois is only thirteen, but it doesn't take her long to figure out[5] that Cappie is not including herself in any of this. By *we* she means Lois. She is accusing Lois of pushing Lucy off the cliff. The unfairness of this hits her like a slap[6]. "I didn't!" she says.

"Didn't what?" says Cappie softly. "Didn't what, Lois?"

Lois does the worst thing, she begins to cry. Cappie gives her a look like a pounce[7]. She's got what she wanted.

Later, when she was grown up, Lois was able to understand what this interview had been about. She could see Cappie's desperation, her need for a story, a real story with a reason in it; anything but the senseless vacancy[8] Lucy had left for her to deal with[9]. Cappie wanted Lois to supply[10] the reason,

1 **have been erased:** tinham sido apagadas • 2 **angry:** com raiva • 3 **without meaning to:** sem querer • 4 **we lose our tempers:** perdemos as estribeiras • 5 **to figure out:** se dar conta • 6 **slap:** bofetada • 7 **Cappie gives her a look like a pounce:** Cappie lançou um olhar fulminante na direção dela • 8 **the senseless vacancy:** o vazio sem sentido • 9 **to deal with:** lidar com • 10 **to supply:** fornecer

to be the reason. It wasn't even for the newspapers or the parents, because she could never make such an accusation without proof[1]. It was for herself: something to explain the loss of Camp Manitou and of all she had worked for, the years of entertaining spoiled[2] children and buttering up[3] parents and making a fool of herself with feathers stuck[4] in her hair. Camp Manitou was in fact lost. It did not survive.

Lois worked all this out[5], twenty years later. But it was far too late. It was too late even ten minutes afterwards, when she'd left Cappie's office and was walking slowly back to her cabin to pack. Lucy's clothes were still there, folded on the shelves, as if waiting. She felt the other girls in the cabin watching her with speculation in their eyes. *Could she have done it? She must have done it.* For the rest of her life, she has caught[6] people watching her in this way.

Maybe they weren't thinking this. Maybe they were merely sorry for her. But she felt she had been tried and sentenced[7], and this is what has stayed with her: the knowledge that she had been singled out[8], condemned for something that was not her fault.

Lois sits in the living room of her apartment, drinking a cup of tea. Through the knee-to-ceiling window she has a wide view of Lake Ontario, with its skin of wrinkled[9]

1 **without proof:** sem provas • 2 **spoiled:** mimadas • 3 **buttering up:** bajulando • 4 **stuck:** enfiadas • 5 **worked all this out:** entendeu tudo isso • 6 **she has caught:** percebeu • 7 **tried and sentenced:** julgada e sentenciada • 8 **singled out:** marcada • 9 **wrinkled:** enrugada

blue-grey light, and of the willows[1] of Centre Island shaken[2] by a wind, which is silent at this distance, and on this side of the glass. When there isn't too much pollution she can see the far shore[3], the foreign shore; though today it is obscured[4].

Possibly she could go out, go downstairs, do some shopping; there isn't much in the refrigerator. The boys say she doesn't get out enough. But she isn't hungry, and moving, stirring[5] from this space, is increasingly an effort.

She can hardly remember, now, having her two boys in the hospital, nursing[6] them as babies; she can hardly remember getting married, or what Rob looked like. Even at the time she never felt she was paying full attention. She was tired a lot, as if she was living not one life but two: her own, and another, shadowy[7] life that hovered[8] around her and would not let itself be realized—the life of what would have happened if Lucy had not stepped sideways[9], and disappeared from time.

She would never go up north, to Rob's family cottage[10] or to any place with wild lakes[11] and wild trees and the calls[12] of loons. She would never go anywhere near. Still, it was as if she was always listening for another voice, the voice of a person who should have been there but was not. An echo.

While Rob was alive, while the boys were growing up, she could pretend she didn't hear it, this empty space in sound. But now there is nothing much left to distract her.

1 **willows:** salgueiros • 2 **shaken:** sacudidos • 3 **the far shore:** a margem oposta • 4 **it is obscured:** não se vê • 5 **stirring:** movimentar-se • 6 **nursing:** amamentar • 7 **shadowy:** nebulosa; enigmática • 8 **hovered:** perseguia • 9 **had not stepped sideways:** não tivesse dado esse passo de lado • 10 **cottage:** chalé • 11 **wild lakes:** lagos agrestes • 12 **calls:** gritos

She turns away from the window and looks at her pictures. There is the pinkish island, in the lake, with the intertwisted[1] trees. It's the same landscape they paddled through, that distant summer. She's seen travelogues[2] of this country, aerial photographs; it looks different from above, bigger, more hopeless: lake after lake, random blue puddles[3] in dark green bush[4], the trees like bristles[5].

How could you ever find anything there, once it was lost? Maybe if they cut it all down, drained it all away[6], they might find Lucy's bones, some time, wherever they are hidden. A few bones, some buttons, the buckle[7] from her shorts.

But a dead person is a body; a body occupies space, it exists somewhere. You can see it; you put it in a box and bury[8] it in the ground, and then it's in a box in the ground. But Lucy is not in a box, or in the ground. Because she is nowhere definite, she could be anywhere.

And these paintings are not landscape paintings. Because there aren't any landscapes up there, not in the old, tidy[9] European sense, with a gentle hill[10], a curving river, a cottage, a mountain in the background[11], a golden evening sky. Instead there's a tangle[12], a receding maze[13], in which you can become lost almost as soon as you step off[14] the path. There are no backgrounds in any of these paintings, no vistas; only a great deal of foreground[15] that goes back and back, endlessly,

1 **intertwisted:** entrelaçadas • 2 **travelogues:** documentários de viagem • 3 **random blue puddles:** poças azuis aleatórias • 4 **bush:** mata • 5 **bristles:** cerdas • 6 **drained it all away:** se drenassem tudo • 7 **buckle:** fivela • 8 **bury:** enterrar • 9 **tidy:** ordenado • 10 **a gentle hill:** uma colina suave • 11 **background:** ao fundo • 12 **tangle:** emaranhado • 13 **a receding maze:** um labirinto que retrocede • 14 **you step off:** você se afasta • 15 **foreground:** primeiro plano

involving you in its twists and turns[1] of tree and branch and rock. No matter how far back in you go[2], there will be more. And the trees themselves are hardly[3] trees; they are currents of energy, charged with violent color.

Who knows how many trees there were on the cliff just before Lucy disappeared? Who counted? Maybe there was one more, afterwards.

Lois sits in her chair and does not move. Her hand with the cup is raised halfway to her mouth. She hears something, almost hears it: a shout of recognition, or of joy.

She looks at the paintings, she looks into them. Every one of them is a picture of Lucy. You can't see her exactly, but she's there, in behind the pink stone island or the one behind that. In the picture of the cliff she is hidden by the clutch of fallen rocks towards the bottom[4], in the one of the river shore she is crouching beneath the overturned canoe[5]. In the yellow autumn woods she's behind the tree that cannot be seen because of the other trees, over beside the blue sliver[6] of pond[7]; but if you walked into the picture and found the tree, it would be the wrong one, because the right one would be further on.

Everyone has to be somewhere, and this is where Lucy is. She is in Lois's apartment, in the holes that open inwards[8] on the wall, not like windows but like doors. She is here. She is entirely alive.

1 **twists and turns:** voltas • 2 **no matter how far back in you go:** não importa até onde você adentra • 3 **hardly:** dificilmente • 4 **the clutch of fallen rocks towards the bottom:** o acúmulo de rochas que caíram para o fundo • 5 **she is crouching beneath the overturned canoe:** está agachada debaixo da canoa virada • 6 **sliver:** pedaço • 7 **pond:** lagoa • 8 **inwards:** por dentro

1ª **edição** fevereiro de 2011 | **Diagramação** Patrícia De Michelis
Fonte Bembo e Berthold Akzidenz Grotesk | **Papel** Chamois 75 g/m²
Impressão e acabamento Yangraf